LETTERS FROM SECLUSION

Forgiveness is a Choice

By Rick Gabriel

Copyright © 2016

Cover Design by: Laura Shinn
Designs

PART 1

Starting

Anew

Dear Son,

It's been many years since I've seen or heard from you. I tried calling but you never picked up your phone. I sent you text messages with no response. I don't have an address for you, since you moved away and sold your home without my knowledge or consent.

The last time I tried to text you, I finally received a message back. Unfortunately, it was from someone else asking me who I was and why I was bothering them. It seems you disconnected your cell phone and disappeared.

I searched for months, then years, trying to find you. I was desperate for some answers, so I thought I'd try a familiar place, the old neighborhood where you grew up. By luck, I came across Kelly, an old friend of yours. I don't know why Kelly knew where you went, but I thanked God for the hope of finding you.

It took me several attempts to convince Kelly to give me a physical address so I could send you a snail mail letter. I pray I didn't waste my time writing.

I don't understand why you abandoned your family and friends. What did we all do to make you want to live so far away? A man doesn't pack up and leave everything he knows unless he's running from extreme circumstances.

All I ask is please respond to my letter. I need to know that you're safe and doing well. A mother needs to know.

Love always,

Mother

Dear Kelly,

We've been friends for many years. I appreciate everything you've done for me through the years. I can still remember the day you found me after my car accident when no one else seemed to care. I'm sure they all hoped I died in the crash. I'm not sure I would have survived if you hadn't found my car in the ditch with me trapped inside.

Seeing your face through the broken glass was like peering at an angel. At that moment, I knew I would be ok. The doctor told me there was a slim chance I would have the use of my legs again. It took many months of recovery through doctor's offices and physical therapy. Thanks to your excellent care, I was able to walk again.

I will always be grateful for that and other countless times you supported me when no one else could be bothered. It was clear I was a burden to my family, even during dire tragedy.

However, I have to say, I'm distraught you told my wicked mother where I am. I talked to you in private about my moving away. You were sworn to secrecy. I trusted you. Where do you get off giving her my address? It's none of her business where I am.

Her letter sounded as if she was loving and supportive, as anyone would expect from a mother. The truth is she has always resented my existence. She hated the day I was born. I guess after having four other children, I was one too many.

I hope you haven't blabbed to the whole world about this. It's embarrassing enough to discuss it with you.

Your Best Friend,

Rich

Dear Rich,

It was good to hear from you after all this time. If only your letter wasn't so harsh. I never have a mean-spirited thing to say to you, even when you lash out at me. Believe me, it's not easy.

I want to thank you for remembering that hard time during your accident. My heart went in my throat when I arrived on scene and saw you bloody and trapped inside your car. I wanted to grab your hand and take all the pain away. I was more than honored to help you recover from that difficult time.

It's true, we've been through a lot together, and I wouldn't trade a moment of it for anything. Still today, you can come to me when you need me. I will always be your friend. Good friends like you are hard to find.

I must clarify one thing. I didn't tell your mother everything we discussed. I only gave her your mailing address because she hounded me for weeks about it. Unable to swallow any more of her nagging, I relented. I promise,

8

the only information she got from me was your address.

I think you owe your mother and your entire family an explanation about why you left. If you don't want to tell them where you went, at least give them that much.

I look forward to hearing from you again,

Kelly

Kelly,

I imagine hearing your voice while reading your comments. You always have a gentle way of getting through to me. This time will be different. I don't owe the woman who gave birth to me anything. She made the decision to pawn me off on a perfect stranger and then act like she's a saint for doing so.

You don't know what it's like being the only member of your family who is treated like an outcast. This may seem angry to you, but there's a good reason for that…I am angry. There's only so much abandoning and back stabbing a man can take in one lifetime. I'm only asking you to understand where I'm coming from.

There's a reason I chose to live in seclusion with no phone, and only public internet (on the rare occasion, I go into town to surf the net). People can't find me, which means people can't hurt me. I don't regret my decision. I went seeking peace in my life and I found it.

The walls here may be dark, but not as grim as my past. I've been through failed relationships and friendships. My entire family hates me. So, why would I want to be around all that negativity again?

I hope you understand,

Rich

My best friend, Rich,

My deepest prayer is that you find the peace the Lord has intended in your life. I'm glad you found somewhere you can call home. My concern is: have you really found peace or are you running away from your issues with your mother? I don't want to sound negative, but I want you to look deep inside yourself for the truth.

Truth is a difficult topic to understand. Many of us only accept truth based on what we can see. It's logical thinking, but it's the opposite of faith. The Bible teaches us to see with our hearts instead of our eyes. So, I want to invite you to close your eyes and ask God what His plan is for your life.

On another point, I find it hard to believe your entire family hates you. Hate is a strong word I wouldn't use lightly. If only you had a father in your life. Any decent man would have stuck around. I didn't know your father very well, and it's just as well from what I hear. The point is, a true father wouldn't want all this

12

dissention between the family members.

As far as backstabbing goes, that's not something you will ever receive from me. If I have ever hurt you, I urge you to let me know. That's the last thing I want to do. You're my lifelong friend and I don't want that to ever change.

I can only encourage you to make an effort to forgive those who hurt you. I can't force it on you. Understand I'm only saying these things because I care too much to keep my mouth shut. I don't want to see you miss the life God has in store for you.

Your life is in His hands,

Kelly

My Dearest Son,

I see you have no interest in responding to my letter. I hate the idea of never hearing from you again. I've spent so much time away from you. Why can't this end?

I know it was my choice to give you up for adoption, but I had to. I was young and inexperienced. I, not only wanted to experience life, but needed to see what life had to offer. Don't you see? This wasn't a selfish choice. I couldn't be the mother you deserved to have, so I did what was best for you.

Your four sisters ask about you all the time. They want to know the whereabouts of their youngest sibling. They all miss you as I do. A big piece of the family puzzle is missing.

It's especially difficult during the holidays. Christmas comes and what used to be the five of you, suddenly was the four of you. Even after several holiday seasons, the emptiness is still there. That will never change until you come home where you belong.

I don't want to seem desperate, but I really am. I simply can't give up on finding you. The address I have for you doesn't come up on my GPS, so the only choice I have is writing again.

I beg you to respond,

Mother

LETTERS FROM SECLUSION

Kelly,

That woman who gave birth to me wrote again.
The hounding I'm enduring from you two is more
than overwhelming. I told you before, I want to be
left alone. I'm not interested in mending a
relationship that never formed in the first place.

Furthermore, the mention of that "god" of yours is
enough to make me vomit. If he's so powerful and
all knowing, why did he let this happen to me? I
didn't deserve to be placed in home after home
with parents who never wanted me. Foster care
was the pits. The experiences I have there are far
too many to count. I might add, none of which
were pleasant.

Another thing that irks me is your comment about
the truth. If you think I'm so incapable of figuring
out what's fact or fiction, why would you keep in
touch with me? Aren't I intelligent enough to
know what's real and what isn't? Why would you
want to have a friend like me? I'm obviously
worthless to the whole world.

That brings me back to where we started. I love
being alone without turmoil or bitterness. It's
brought out a part in me I never knew I had.
Believe it or not, this is a beneficial experience.
I'm striving and will never go back to my old way

FORGIVENESS IS A CHOICE

of life. It was toxic and I don't need that…no one does.

I'm just asking you to understand,

Rich

Rich,

I understand your point of view and want nothing more than to support you as a good friend. Everyone has their faults and shortcomings. I'm far from perfect. Scripture makes it clear, "We all have sinned and fallen short of the glory found in Christ Jesus."

You may not like hearing my talk about God. The bitterness in your heart about Him shines through your writing. There was a time I didn't understand who Jesus is. If you will open yourself up to hearing about my experiences, I would love to tell you about them.

It hurts me to see you so angry. There were many years when we spent hours laughing and having fun. I didn't see any bitterness in you then. It took time for you to

reveal the pain inside you.
I don't recall when I first
noticed it, but I knew your
issues were severe.

Suppose we did this: You
open up about your past and I
will listen, so I can get a
complete picture of what
you're hiding from the world.
It will be in complete
confidence. In return, I
will tell you the deepness in
me you may not know, even
after our long history.

Don't think, ever, that I was
saying you aren't
intelligent. That's not, at
all, how I feel. I have deep
respect for you. Telling
yourself that you are
worthless isn't going to help
your situation; it will only
make things worse. You will
always believe the things you
let out of your mouth. So,
try telling yourself you are
special in His sight. I
think you're special too. If

only you thought that about yourself and realized you are deeply loved, the walls you've built up around you could vanish.

I don't think anyone truly wants to be alone. Some may choose that path because it seems the easier road. In reality, people are everywhere, so you can't run for long. They will always find you, even if they aren't looking.

Let's talk more about this soon,

Kelly

Kelly,

I know I should have written sooner, but I needed time to think about what to say. I read your last letter a dozen times, it seems. I had to ponder your words and let them sink in. My initial thought was you really insulted me. Then I crumpled the letter and threw it away. After a few days I took it out of the trash and read it again.

I realized I was being selfish and immature. I can't turn my back on my only friend. When I decided to live in seclusion, I made a vow to myself to never accept hurtful words from anyone again. Now, you've made me rethink that idea. Maybe there are walls built up around me. I'm at a loss of how to break them down.

I'm not saying everything you said was right. The point you made about "We have all sinned and fallen short" is more than questionable. Who has the right to label me a sinner? I think when a man has "fallen" as many times and many ways as I have, he has a right to seek out an alternative way of life.

If you think about it, the things that happened to me aren't my fault. So why am I a sinner? It sounds like you're trying to say being pushed away by people who are supposed to be my family is because of my erroneous actions. I'd like to think this isn't the case, since I know you. I'm hoping you will clarify.

I'm not sure I can talk about my past. I need some time to enjoy being me, without having to conform to the world's standards. I spent my whole life letting others manipulate my decisions. That part of me is gone. It will never surface again.

If you want to talk about your past, go right ahead. I will listen and try to be objective. Don't get your hopes up with me. I'm not fit for this world, so don't expect me to open up. The thought of listening to you talk about your childhood, or wherever you were in your life when you decided Jesus was real, isn't going to be easy to swallow. All I can say is I will listen as a friend.

I look forward to hearing from you,

Rich

My closest friend, Rich,

I'm encouraged to hear back from
you so quickly. I was wondering
if you decided to shut me out.
I'm glad I was wrong. The several
weeks you didn't write left an
indescribable void in me. I thank
God for your friendship. It warms
my heart that, even during your
time away, you found it necessary
to keep our relationship intact.

The last letter you sent had a
much different feel. I didn't
sense the anger you have displayed
in the past. I'm hoping and
praying you will find my words
encouraging as yours encouraged
me.

On the discussion about sinners,
it's not a simple answer. Many of
life's questions about faith and
what God is all about aren't easy.
That's why God gave us His own
Word. The answers to who He is
and why He created us is written
there in black and white...along
with some red letters to represent
Jesus' words (in some Bibles).

After all you've been through,
it's understandable why you built
barriers around you. There were

many years I thought I would never trust another pastor, priest, or church again. What I'm about to tell you left me bitter. I couldn't even talk about it or think about it without feeling hatred toward God. If you remember the first time we talked about my faith in Jesus, I told you I used to be an atheist. I wasn't interested in talking about why at the time, but I'm ready now.

Going to church was an every Sunday ritual in my house. It was as far back as I can remember. My mother got me up at 8am. Everyone left the house in fancy clothes. It was the only time my mother put on makeup, and she fussed to put on the church face. Dad had on his jacket and tie.

I have to roll my eyes every time I think about him looking like the well put together father and husband. He was a church worker. Everyone adored him. The men went to him for advice about marriage and raising kids. All along he was cheating on my mother.

I saw the signs. He fought with my mother on a regular basis. It was like they were roommates rather than husband and wife. Even at an early age, I could see there was something wrong in their relationship.

There was a time when they always kissed and held hands. I don't know if after several years being married made their love fade...or I should ask: What made their love fade? The point is, they seem to take each other for granted and did nothing but get on each other's nerves.

My older sister, Kristen, never suspected anything was amiss. One morning, as we were getting ready for school, my dad came to my mom and tried to be affectionate to her in the kitchen. This was a rare occurrence at this point. She turned away and made the excuse she had to get ready for work. Kristen started laughing as if she was watching a sitcom.

I only looked down at my breakfast cereal, as to be oblivious of the situation. Inside I knew it was the beginning of the end of their

24

marriage. I was right. Within a week or two, my father told both Kristen and me that he was leaving. He didn't mention why.

I would have never expected an affair from the man I thought was beyond err. After he was gone a couple of months, I learned he was with another woman. I didn't know how to take the news at the age of 12. I didn't believe it at first. In fact, I had to talk to my dad to inform him of the rumors my mother was spreading about him.

I asked dad to pick me up from school, so we could talk. He seemed excited to spend time with me. I heard an excitement in his voice, over the phone, I hadn't heard in a long time. It was a bittersweet afternoon.

As he pulled his Rolls Royce in front of the main entrance, I saw an unforgettable smile on his face. My agenda was the last thing on his mind. I hopped in shot gun and he promptly hugged me, as if he hadn't seen me for 50 years. I cried as he told me he missed me and loved me.

FORGIVENESS IS A CHOICE

This next part is challenging. I had to walk away from this letter for a while as I collected my thoughts. I hope you're ready because it's not pleasant.

We went to *The Three Amigos*. Yes, he took me to a nice Mexican restaurant. It was his idea. As he said, I was worth it. I must admit we had a nice visit and the food was incredible. Dad made me laugh and smile.

He brought up things I did years earlier that he thought was cute. I saw the joy in his face as he talked. It tells me he holds his memories of me and my sister close to his heart. For the moment, I found myself in familiar territory, close to my dad.

This only made the anxiety rise as I anticipated bringing up his affair. I took a deep breath and looked high at the ceiling. Dad asked me what was bothering me. The response I gave him was vague. I'm not sure how I put it, but I held back tears as I began to talk.

Dad held my hand as he continued. I'll never forget the harsh, yet

26

worried look on his face. He squinted with skepticism and asked me to tell him what was on my mind.

After a minute or two, I looked into his eyes, and told him mom had said he was seeing another woman. The response he gave me shattered my view of him forever. He confirmed the rumors and admitted to his crimes. He was having an affair. It was true. He was unfaithful.

I spent many months with bitterness toward my mother. I thought for sure she made up the story to make herself look like the innocent victim. I hoped that was the case when I visited with my dad.

A pain seeped deep inside my heart. I couldn't believe it was true. He really was sleeping with a young girl behind everyone's back. In a way, I understood why he wanted another woman. My mother was horrible to him: verbally abusive, gossiped about him...even to her own children. Now I had to sort out why he would do this and leave his own flesh and blood.

Sure, I made excuses for him. That's what all good children should do. The truth is, he made this decision on his own and he didn't think about anyone but himself. The man I looked up to my whole life made the worst decision of his life…at least as far as I'm concerned.

A moment of awkward silence turned the nice visit we were having into the worst day of my life. I didn't know how to respond. I couldn't cry and I couldn't get mad. An invisible sword penetrated my soul and sucked the life out of me.

I got up and walked out of the restaurant, not knowing how I would get home. That was furthest from my mind. Dad ran out after me and begged me to come back inside. I refused and reached for my cell phone in my purse. He grabbed my hand to prevent me from using it. Begging again, he pulled me toward the entrance to the restaurant.

LETTERS FROM SECLUSION

Anger dwelt up and I pushed him off me. I'll never forget my words to him, "Get off me you two-faced, poor excuse of a human being!" Dad shook his head as others stared. When he persisted, I pushed him again and again. Finally, he got the idea and backed off. I ran off in tears he didn't deserve.

The days went by and I didn't call him. Every time my phone rang, anxiety dwelt in me as I hoped it wasn't him on the other end. I couldn't focus on school or my friends. Sleeping was impossible, most nights. I shut down from everyone.

Going to church was out of the question. I didn't want to see him playing the well put together Christian icon. It was enough to make me stab him. Our pastor confronted me and asked me why he hadn't seen me in a few weeks. My mother tried to guilt me into going. I couldn't sit there every Sunday and wear a fake smile when the inside of me was destroyed.

What followed was the biggest mistake I could have made. The years went by and time didn't heal my wounds. I became an adult and ran as far away from God as I could. It's embarrassing to admit, but I was stupid enough to turn to drugs, alcohol, and one bad relationship after another.

Just when I thought this new lifestyle was the perfect escape route, I had a run in with the law. I got arrested on drug charges and was forced into a treatment center. I knew I needed help and the Holy Spirit was working on me, even though I didn't know it.

I requested a Christian based program only because it was familiar. I knew I was being thrown into an uncomfortable environment with people I didn't know, where I couldn't get high or drunk. The only thing I felt at that moment was fear, and a lot of it.

After 72 days of being clean and working through the 12-step program, I learned how to accept life as it comes. I had to cut off contact with toxic people.

LETTERS FROM SECLUSION

Otherwise I would end up back on the road to destruction.

This all may sound cliché to you, but it's the truth. It was hard to write and admit this embarrassing part of me, but I can honestly say I'm a survivor. Yes, it was a challenging time and I put a lot of work into it, but I couldn't have done it without God's help. He gave me the wisdom to choose a Christian rehab instead of a secular one, at a time when I couldn't have been more mad at God.

In the end, I can only say, He did it for me and He can do the same for you. He won't force you, so you have to give it to Him. He loves you even if it doesn't feel that way.

I've talked enough for one letter, so I'll let you soak all this in. My prayer is you will understand we all have our struggles. No one is exempt.

I look forward to your response,

Kelly

FORGIVENESS IS A CHOICE

My Son,

I hate to sound harsh, but I think this has gone on long enough. You can't ignore your mother forever. I am the only biological mother you will ever have. If you still can't understand why I couldn't raise you, I can't help that.

I miss you and never forgot about you. I was in tears as I saw your sweet face for the last time, as a baby. I didn't even know if I would ever see you again. It's a time that will apparently haunt me the rest of my life. I don't even know what to say anymore.

You should say hello to your siblings. What have they done to you? It wasn't their choice to give you up for adoption. Don't you see there are people who love you?

I hope you respond. Your family needs you,

Mother

LETTERS FROM SECLUSION

Loving Rich,

It's been years since we spoke. Being the oldest, I thought it was important that I write on behalf of myself and our other three siblings. As much as I hate to speak for other people, I think you need to know how much you are loved.

I can only imagine what you went through living in foster care. I've heard all the stories from mom. She wishes she can take it all back. You may not think it's true, but mom loves you and wants to connect with you. Please find it in yourself to, at least, write to her.

Living by yourself has to be rough. No one really wants to be alone. There may be people who chose to live without the contact of others, but they can't be happy.

This may sound like a bunch of hogwash to you, but please believe me. I need to hear your voice and laugh with you again. You bring the gift of laughter to so many, it's a shame to waste it.

Your many nieces and nephews are missing their uncle. Have you thought about how different life would be without them? Has living alone solved all your problems? I'm only trying to get you to think.

Your Oldest Sibling,

Danielle

FORGIVENESS IS A CHOICE

Kelly,

I'm so overwhelmed with letters from my annoying family, I don't know where to start. This whole thing started when you gave my mailing address to that woman who gave me up for adoption. I'm sorry for attacking you, but I wish you kept your promise of secrecy.

Not only am I getting mail from mom, but now my oldest sibling. I came here to get away from all the hounding and constant adversity. Now I feel like I need to run away from my new life. When is this going to stop?

I value your friendship, so don't feel like I want to push you away. I did read and ponder your last letter, so don't think I'm ignoring it.

The story of your father is shocking. Affairs happen all the time. I don't know how people can justify having one. There was a time I didn't think it was a big problem. I've heard of marriages that survive an affair, but I can't think it will ever be healthy again. How can you trust your partner after they betrayed your trust?

As shocked as I was at your father's behavior, it was nothing compared to hearing about your addiction and rehab. Wow! You seem to be so proper and even flawless. I've always looked up

34

to you and after hearing this, I think I respect you even more. I'm glad it worked out for you.

I wish I was the type of person who can overcome such obstacles. Some can handle life's "challenges," as they say, and others have to hide them. I got tired of pretending everything was ok. It was killing me inside.

I must admit I ran to alcohol while I was around my, so called, family. I couldn't handle the pain, so I started drinking. I have a love for margaritas. In fact, I liked them too much, to the point where I was drunk every night before going to bed. It felt good. I was happy. The hurt transformed into a strength I never had before. It was like a superhero taking off his disguise to reveal his powerful identity.

All was good until my sibling, closest to my age, came into my home without my knowledge or consent. I must have left the door unlocked. This snake slithered her way into the living room, where I was sitting, and saw me laying on the couch. I could barely see it was her through blurred vision. I think she crept her way in from the crack under the door, as a sidewinder burrows through the sand.

I must have dozed off, because I could only hear her talking on the phone. She stated my address in a hurried manner and said I was passed out with alcohol poisoning. It was, of course, a lie. I couldn't have been passed out if I heard her and she had no idea if I had alcohol poisoning. She's not a doctor.

The next thing I remember is looking up and seeing a cluster of strangers around me. They all wore hospital garb. I was in a partially elevated position, unable to lay flat. An attractive woman turned to me, flipping her curly brunette hair partially in her face. She smiled and looked at me with deep brown eyes.

I looked around to see curtains all around me, but no one I knew, including that slithering sibling who put me there. She didn't even have the guts to face me. If I was so sick, why didn't my family come to my aid? Isn't that what family is supposed to do? That's why I know they don't want me around.

I had a blood pressure cuff on one arm, an IV in the opposite hand, and an oxygen mask on my face. That wasn't the worst part. Someone shoved an endotracheal tube down my throat. Good grief! Did I drink too much or have a heart attack? This wouldn't have happened if my sister kept her nose out of my business.

The pretty brunette told me she was the doctor and asked me how I was feeling. I couldn't answer with a tube in my mouth, so I shook my head at her. Then she put a pencil in my hand and asked me to write down my responses. She asked me a bunch of questions, most of which were insulting. I felt like a criminal in front of a judge.

In the end, she told me she was giving me medication to help me relax. I could see my blood pressure on the monitor was elevated. I actually was afraid at that point. I didn't know whether the medical staff was trying to kill me or keep me alive. There's no one out there I trust.

I stayed in that room for a few hours, and then was moved to a private room. I didn't care as long as they took that dumb tube out of my mouth. At least I could breathe on my own. It didn't take long for me to fall asleep.

When I woke up, I was still alone. My family never visited me until it was time for me to go home. A person at the hospital offered me a rehab center in town, but I refused. That's ridiculous since I only ended up there because of my meddlesome sister.

On the way home, the woman who gave birth to me told me I was out of control and a bunch of other degrading things I didn't need to hear. I was sick and weak. She just made me sicker. Naturally, it didn't occur to her, all the nagging is what made me drink in the first place.

I was never so glad to be home, even if it was close to two of those depressing siblings. At least I wasn't close to mom. I wouldn't buy a house close to her in a drunken stupor.

Anyway, that's enough of my rambling. I'm just upset all over again. I hate hearing from those idiots.

You can write any time.

Your Best Friend,

Rich

My Dearest Rich,

Even in the harshest of times, it's good to hear from you. Something about seeing your name on an envelope brightens my day.

I wasn't sure how you would take to my rehab experience. I had to laugh when you described me as "flawless." Allow me to clarify. I'm far from perfect. I only serve a God who is without flaw (to use your words). He's more powerful than my struggles.

I don't know if an apology is in order for giving your address to your mother, but I want to say it anyway. I didn't mean to cause you any more emotional struggles. You've been through so much in your life, my heart aches for you. If there was any way I could take it all away, I would.

Now that we've gotten to talk about hard stuff, I want to say how proud I am. You discussed an episode in the past I didn't know, just when I thought I knew everything about you. It takes courage to admit something that embarrassing. I have a million

FORGIVENESS IS A CHOICE

stories to trade if you're interested.

It seems the subject of your family is a bitter one. I hate to bring it up, but I care for you too much not to mention it. We all have different backgrounds which molds us into the person God wants us to be. Trust me when I say, The Lord understands your struggles more than you do.

I want you to consider writing someone in your family. It doesn't have to be your mother. It may be hard, but consider how they've made an effort to connect with you.

Gently yours,

Kelly

LETTERS FROM SECLUSION

My brother, Rich,

The family waited a few weeks to no avail. It's obvious you aren't interested in responding to Danielle's and Mom's letters. So, here goes my attempt, hopefully not for nothing. I'm not trying to bug you. It's just the opposite. I want to respect your privacy and help you understand where I'm coming from.

I don't want to say anything to upset you, so I'll start with some curious questions. What's it like where you are? Is life really different? I don't know where you are specifically and I won't ask. Is it really quiet there? I want to get a picture of your environment. That's the only reason I ask.

It's hard, talking to you this way. The nights for me are the hardest. I sit outside, after the kids are in bed, and look up at the stars. It's a

41

peaceful sight, but lonesome. Do you remember when we used to lay there and try to count the stars? I told you it was impossible. You insisted there was a way. I think that was the night I learned to laugh out loud. Your futile counting led to the depths of our relationship.

I didn't know you that well, but it would soon change. Since I'm so much younger than our older siblings, they ignored me most of the time. I don't blame them. I was the one who tattled on them. They didn't want me to know anything in fear of my telling mom. It was hurtful being left out, but you filled the void.

I remember when mom bought you that telescope and we began studying the constellations. You were so excited when you found

Orion's belt, then the rest of his body, including his sword and bow. You told me about the two dogs, Canis Major and Canis Minor, who accompanied him while hunting. You pretended to be Orion and tried to sword down Lepus the rabbit and Taurus the Bull.

I know it was a long time ago, but I'll never forget how much joy you brought me. I never knew a young girl could laugh so much.

It all went sour when you had to go back to your foster home. That was the pits. I had to hold back tears in front of others. It got old quick. The school week went so slow, but knowing I would see you again on the weekend gave me something to look forward to.

The day I found out you were going to live with foster parents hit me hard. It was like someone jabbed me with a knife, and the inner part of me that knew how to enjoy life, was stripped away. I went back to being ignored by my older sisters.

I couldn't wait until you became an adult. You could get out there and make a life for yourself. I pictured you in a shirt and tie, working in an office. That did happen, but you were too busy for me. We grew up and our lives changed.

You got involved with that woman at the office with the perfect figure (I shake my head as I think about it). You know I never liked her, which is why I had to stop you from pursuing a relationship with her. She was manipulative and really didn't care about you. I know you don't see it that way, but I didn't want you getting hurt.

LETTERS FROM SECLUSION

After you and I had the big argument over it, you seemed to hold it against me. I was trying to help because I love you. The remainder is hard to talk about, so I won't bring it up.

I'll close for now because I'm feeling down. I miss you a lot and hope you will finally reach out to your sister.

Your Youngest Sibling,

Rebecca

Kelly,

Like I said before, I value our friendship. You are the only person who hasn't betrayed me. Although, I'm still pondering the fact that you broke my trust when you gave my address to the woman who gave birth to me. Now everyone in my family has been bothering me.

I got a letter from another sister. That's family member number 3 now. Is it never going to stop? She brought up ugly stuff from the past as well as times when we got along okay. I guess she thinks that's supposed to make up for all the damage she caused me.

I don't know how you can say you're proud of me. I've never accomplished anything in my life. No one wants me within 2000 miles of them. All my friends have turned on me, except you. My career is over because I quit my job and moved away. You really need to re-evaluate that word you used: proud.

I'm going to have to stop writing for a while, until I can figure out what I should do about all this. I came here to protect myself from all the crap my family did to me. Now I'm not so sure this is going to work. I hate the thought of moving again, but it seems that's the only way I can escape the hounding letters.

Don't take it personally,

Rich

Lovely best friend, Rich,

I don't take it lightly when you talk about shutting me out, like everyone else. The world is a cruel place and we have to embrace life. That's what God expects from us. You would benefit from the never ending good news, found in His Word.

You've said several times my talking about God and the Bible makes you ill. It saddens me when I think about you going through life without Him. The things I say may bother you, but you need to hear them. Sorry if I come across as bossy. That's not my intent, but I must tell you the truth.

As far as re-evaluating my choice of words, I think it's the other way around. The fact that you live over 2000 miles away was a choice you made, not because your loved ones don't want you around.

I really wish you hadn't given up on your career. You were successful and you know it. The company you worked for was worldwide and you received several promotions while working there.

LETTERS FROM SECLUSION

Just for the record, you deserved them. That's why I'm proud of you and brag about you to others.

Before you decide not to write anymore, I want to stress the importance of relationships. I may be your only friend, as you say, but I will always honor your loyalty. It's not by accident that our paths crossed. It's all part of a divine intervention.

I'm honestly worried about you. Leaving everything you know, in my opinion, goes beyond logic. Now you want to retreat once again. Where will you go? I hate to ask, but out of concern, I must know. Don't shut me out. I never want to lose contact.

I don't know what else to say that may convince you to open up to those who love you. I would attempt a visit if I thought it wouldn't upset you. Don't fret; I will honor your wishes by leaving you alone.

Please don't shut me out,

Kelly

Dear Mentor,

I have loved being here, but I'm afraid it's time for me to move on again. I know I just purchased this house in a secluded area of Washington State. There has to be a way to get out of here with the money I put into the house. Even if I can't, it will be worth getting out of here.

My family has been writing me the most annoying letters, blaming me for everything and making themselves out to be a bunch of saints. That really gets under my skin. One thing I can't stand is a bunch of self-righteous morons making themselves out to be gods.

I thought I found the perfect place to call home. Even though it's in a housing development, the house is surrounded by trees and on top a hill. It's perfect. I don't have to worry about anyone bothering me. Peace and quiet is something I have craved all my life. Now it's all being destroyed by the letters.

I will miss hanging out with you. You add wisdom I didn't have before. Your care free lifestyle is why I talk to you. As you know, I don't associate with too many people. You're older and your experience in life has brought you to a good place. If it hadn't been for both our hard lives, we would have never met.

I hope I get to see you over the next few weeks or months, before I move away. When the time comes, I will never forget the fellowship we had.

Little me,

Rich

Young Fella,

Don't be so hasty. I hate to start a conversation like that, but you need to think about what you're giving up. How many times are you going to run away? Your problems will follow you until you decide to conquer them. We've had this discussion before.

Didn't you learn anything from what I said? You mentioned "I add wisdom" to your life. So, why throw all that away? I get it, that you don't want to be around your family. I can't say I blame you and I won't dispute that.

I only have so much time left on this earth. Before I become part of the ground, I want to say I accomplished something in this world. Hopefully, I will make an impact in your life before I go.

After all these years, I never thought I'd find anyone who understood me. You not only understand me, but you have walked in my shoes, in a lot of ways. It's good to know I'm not the only one who was cursed with a horrible, rotten family. Of course, I don't call them family. They are just people who lived in the same house and pretended to care about me out of obligation.

As you, they gave me up for adoption because I hindered them from traveling the world and drinking exotic drinks. The money they spent on my care robbed them of the next cruise line. So, I had to go.

I know you've heard all this over and over, but I'm still really upset. I learned early on not to trust anyone. It took living alone for 50 years to teach me how to trust one person...you. It's a miracle we met, as you say. I must agree with you on that.

I have to laugh as I think about the first time you walked into the tavern. I saw you checking out the bartender. Sheila is young and beautiful. She makes the most in tips in that place because she knows how to turn on the guys. You youngsters are full of hormones you don't know what to do with.

I was sitting at the corner of the bar, as always, and you sat down 3 stools to the right of me. It was smack in the middle of the bar. You ordered your margarita and stuttered as you thanked the bartender. As I laughed, you looked over at me and shook your head.

I could see you didn't want to talk to me or anyone else. So, I teased you about gawking at Sheila. You only nodded your head. Since there weren't many people there that night, I persisted in talking to you. It didn't take long before I got a laugh out of you. Then you finally lightened up and we started a conversation.

It didn't take long for both of us to learn we had much in common. Our childhoods, dating life, friends that came and went out of our lives, and the list goes on. It's scary to think how much we're alike. It was the luck of an old Irishman that brought us together.

So, rethink this moving away thing. Who cares if your family writes you? If it bothers you that much, don't write them back. Better yet, don't even read the letters. Throw them away, unopened.

That's what I did when my "family" tried to contact me.

Think it over for both of our sakes,

Mentor

My Mentor,

It's hard to consider leaving after reading your response. I like our chats and the fact that we share the same backgrounds. I can't imagine finding anyone else like you. Just when I thought my experiences were unique, you helped me see I'm not crazy. It's nice to know someone who understands and validates my point of view.

The house here, I bought with cash, and it was equivalent to the house I sold in Kansas City. I needed no mortgage and have plenty of cash on hand. If I was to move from Washington, finances wouldn't stop me. I searched everywhere for a secluded place with not much population. It's not easy to find.

Excuse me while I take a walk to clear my head. I'm at a loss.

Now that I'm back home, after a couple hours, I can finish our discussion.

While I was out, I pondered a lot of things. The woman who gave birth to me, and then gave me away, was first on my list. She started the letter chain. The thought of talking to her again makes me ill. However, if I decide to contact anyone in my family, it should be my sister, Rebecca. We were close at one time. Then again, she tried to have me put away, like I'm a junkie.

Then there's Danielle, my other sister. She's the oldest of my siblings. I don't know why she would write me. That woman never paid attention to me accept to call me stupid and annoying. This is the thing I hate the most about my family. They all treated me like a second-class citizen and now they want to pretend to care. What's that all about?

As I approached the bottom of the stairs that lead to my front door, covered in trees and bushes, I stopped with one foot on the bottom riser. My body was heavy with the dilemma of my best friend back home. Perhaps I should write and let Kelly know what's going on.

The sun started to fall and I still hadn't mustered enough energy to climb the stairs and go inside. My legs felt like they were 1000 pounds each. I started to cry because I realized there is no escape from my past.

Now that I'm inside, writing at my desk, I feel safe. This house is my security blanket. No one visits me and I don't invite anyone. That's the way I want it. The trees around the house are too thick to see out the windows, which adds to the privacy. Some would say it's like being in prison.

If that's true, at least I'm safe from the outside world's cruelty.

Now that I've decided to stay here in Washington, maybe I'll pop over to the tavern for a few drinks. I could use a bunch of them.

See you soon,

Rich

LETTERS FROM SECLUSION

Young Fella,

It's a relief you want to stay. You would have made a very big mistake.
Sometimes you make rash decisions. I'm glad this time you used your head...at least a little.

I was mad at you at first, but after having a couple beers, I didn't care anymore. I didn't see you until the sun went down. You were too busy walking about and staring at the bottom of your staircase. I used to do things like that, but time has healed my wounds. Life can't hurt me anymore.

This grey hair and beard shows I have wisdom. I'm smart enough and strong enough to push the world away and all its hurts. It's an incredible feeling to know I have the power over all that junk. I have one tool, contained inside a 12 ounce can. Sometimes I splurge for the beer on tap.

It was good to see you when you walked in after dark. We've been meeting here for so long, you didn't need to order your drink. Your favorite bartender was

59

working. She brought you a margarita and you gave her that flirtatious smile, as always.

Maybe you'll brave up enough to talk to her. She may be available. You won't know unless you try. I know you don't hang with many people, but it's just a thought. Love may come your way.

Now, onto a more serious subject. Your best friend in Kansas sounds like a good person. I don't understand why you wouldn't want to keep in touch. It's your call, but I don't see what the problem is if Kelly hasn't hurt you. I don't want to bug you, so I won't say any more about it.

It's getting late for this old man,

Your Faithful Mentor

Mentor,

Last night was fun once I got out of the house and spent some time with you. I didn't realize the need I have to talk to you. As much as I like being alone, it's good to hear your wisdom and encouragement. The depression became overwhelming sitting in the middle of the house, staring at a tree covered window.

A margarita never tasted so good. I may be young, but I know the feeling of a good alcohol buzz. Talk about healing all wounds. It doesn't take a grey beard to heal from the past.

As far as talking to the pretty bartender, you can forget that. I don't need to get involved with another female who will eventually abandon me. Of course, I like to look at her. They're all beautiful until they take advantage of you and dump you for another man. I don't need that crap.

Time has taught me I'm naturally undesirable. Maybe women are interested in the beginning...or I should say, they pretend to be interested.

Apparently, I have a stamp on my forehead saying, "I have money and I'm a sucker." If you're interested in hearing my dating war stories, we could talk for hours, or even days.

I stayed at the tavern after you left last night. I moved to the bar to sit closer to the eye candy. She smiled at me quite a bit, but I didn't engage in a conversation. Perhaps, shyness was the cause. Possibly, it was fear of rejection. Whatever the reason, I couldn't find anything to say to her that didn't pertain to ordering another drink.

The thought of talking to Kelly again crossed my mind. It's hard to fathom life without my best friend from far away. Without the two of you, I don't know what I would do. A heavy sigh emitted from my mouth when I contemplated the many facets of my world.

I bury my face in my hands and shake my head. How am I supposed to keep my relationship with Kelly intact while guarding my heart from more betrayal? There's not another ounce of heartache I can take.

If there was any way to connect with people, I would. It's like I was born on another planet and transported into a land where I don't belong. Others can see me and I can see them, but only through a stain glass window. I'm there, but only look good from the outside.

I'm sure that's what celebrities go through. The big-time movie stars appear to have everything they could want or need. What's on the inside? Are they hurting? Do they hide the parts of them that are missing and unfulfilled? Can millions of dollars make up for all their emptiness?

All I can say is I wouldn't complain so much if I were as rich as them. Money isn't a big issue with me, although I don't make as much money working from home as I did in my last job. It was a good one, but not worth the verbal abuse from my family.

I'll close before I depress myself into an alcoholic coma,

Rich

Rich,

I'm hesitant to write. I pray you haven't left your home to run and hide again. Forgive me for putting it that way. The thought of you has consumed me at work, home, the grocery store, in the car, and everywhere else. We've been friends for a lot of years and I'm not ready to throw it away.

Prayers are going up for you by many people, not just myself. I talked before about a divine intervention and God has you in His hands. You may decide to be alone, but it's not in His plan.

Those 2000 miles that separate us is a speck in His eye. Allow The Lord Jesus to close the gap and bring us back together, even if it has to be through letters again. The power of the pen has ended many conflicts.

Please listen to me. I'm not here to chastise you.

I'm not sure what to say to convince you I'm on your side. I would rather die than hurt you.

LETTERS FROM SECLUSION

My desk is always open when you
want to communicate.

Don't let too much time slide by,

Kelly

Trusted Friend and Mentor,

You're not going to believe this, but Kelly wrote me again. I thought I made it clear I needed time to think this whole thing through. As I roll my eyes, it angers me that no one will respect my wishes.

I know you said I should keep my relationships intact. Maybe I'm being too cold. I don't know. For now, I need to stick to my guns and protect myself from further harm. My life stays inside my little house and nightly treks to the tavern.

Although, we've spent many hours talking and learning from each other, it's obvious there is more to discuss. One thing you said made no sense to me. One minute, you're talking about shutting the world out and the next you're saying Kelly is important. I can't have it both ways unless I split myself in two pieces.

I suppose it doesn't matter. I'm not looking to mend any relationships right now, or ever. My life is simple now and I will keep it that way.

My margarita was waiting for me at our table tonight. It made me smile as I watched another sun fall. You gave me the thumbs up as I plopped in my rickety seat. The joy hits me when I see you and gulp my first hit of alcohol.

I noticed other people staring and making jokes about my nightly visits. It's okay with me, since they are there too. It takes a drunk to know a drunk. I've been called much worse. There's no need to cause a scene that may lead to a fight. I can take sarcasm from deadbeats I don't know and don't like.

It surprised me when you said you would pay for my first drink. Then again, I bought yours when you were down on cash. Sheila slid a second margarita in front of me without my asking. I'd like to think she's been paying attention to me, but I know I'm just another customer who tips a beautiful bartender.

As I sit here with you, the thought of Kelly comes to mind. I won't ponder it too long, since the night is young and conversation is uplifting. Why worry about the world's bitter treatment? Who cares?

Well, the game is about to start, so we'll be shouting and slapping high fives as appropriate. Happy hour is my best friend. Maybe I'll buy a round for our faithful locals. I can splurge once in a while.

Sheila came by and smiled at me without reason. My heart started to pound like a teenager with a crush. Her long brown hair brushed against my face. It gave me a high I couldn't get from a full keg of beer. She looked back at me and smiled again. Obviously, she knows I'm attracted to her. Only a female can lift my spirits along with the plethora of drinks I've had at this point.

Sports helps too. I always fantasize about being a millionaire movie star with women all around me and television cameras in my face. The thought of being that significant is as far from reality as life could be.

Oh well, at least I've learned to get enjoyment out of my disappointing life, as minimal as it may be.

Thanks for good times,

Rich

Jumpy Rich,

I thought you were going to have a heart attack when Sheila started flirting with you. The night is young. Why not go up to her and start a conversation? You're drunk enough, that's for sure. So what if she snubs you? Although, I really don't think she will. Go for it.

The tavern is getting crowded with loud people. That happens every time there's a game on. It's good to sit back and watch the die-hard fans. They're more entertaining than television.

Seeing you finally loosen up and enjoy yourself makes me think all my lecturing wasn't a waste of time. I didn't think you were capable of laughing. Apparently, Sheila lifted your spirits. A good-looking woman will do that.

As much as I hate to bring up, you asked a serious question. *One minute, you're talking about shutting the world out and the next you're saying Kelly is important.* I think shutting the world out helps us protect ourselves from bad people. Everyone is flawed and wants to take advantage of others to feed their selfishness. The point is, I think you have a good person in Kelly who cares about you. It's rare to find.

I've been on planet earth a lot longer than you, but I never found a real friend until now. It's good to have you to fill that vacancy. I couldn't get it from my family and all my friends moved on and forgot about me. That's why I moved here. If no one cares about me, why should I stay in my home town?

I don't want to spoil your good mood, but it wouldn't hurt you to contact Kelly, just to say hi. I don't know this person. As I sit here, I wonder if there's a motive involved, but I can't make that assumption. A letter wouldn't hurt. That's all I'm saying about it.

It's your choice,

The Old Man

Kelly,

It's been a while since I talked to you. I'm sorry I took so long. It took an old guy here to convince me to do so. I think you misunderstood me when I last wrote. The intent wasn't to shut you out. I needed time to clear my head and contemplate this retreat objectively.

The time away from writing has been good for me. I've been spending a lot of time at home during the day and at a nearby tavern at night. Yes, I mean every night. The old guy I just mentioned is the only person I can talk to here…just when I thought there was no one.

Enough about him. I want you to know I have no plans of leaving Washington or selling my home. It's taken me this long to start getting comfortable here. My house is perfect for me and I can relax with a few margaritas in the evening to forget about my past.

I'm sure you're going to continue to ask me to write to my family. As I've told you, there's nothing to talk about on the subject. I wouldn't even know what to say to them, except harsh words.

I want to thank you again for caring enough to keep in touch and not giving up on our friendship.

71

FORGIVENESS IS A CHOICE

It means more to me than I can say. However, I have to say I still don't know how you can believe in a "god" who caused so much pain. Why should I want to be a part of that? If there is a god out there, he doesn't care about me. I would even say, he hates me.

I would like to know who all these people are who are supposedly praying for me. Maybe someone told you that, but I'm sure it's a lie. People say lots of things they don't mean. They only do things to benefit themselves. If there's money to be made, I would become an Eskimo and sell ice cubes for a living.

Therefore, I don't want to talk to that woman who gave birth to me or any of her other children who were good enough for her to keep. I just get mad all over again. It's not worth the ulcers. Forget it.

You can write anytime,

Rich

Rich,

I don't know if hearing from your youngest sister is doing good or harm to you. There's lots I want to talk to you about. If only you would respond to me. It hurts to the bone that you want nothing to do with me.

I assume you're still mad at me for calling that ambulance. It scared me when I came in your house to find you unconscious on the couch. I knew you had been drinking because you always drink after work, and also there were empty containers around the living room.

I didn't do it out of spite or to control you. I want you to live your life, but I love you too much to let you die. Something tells me I called in good time. The doctor in the hospital told me you were lucky.

I never want to see you that close to death again.

Let's move on to another subject. Last night after I put the kids to bed and kissed my husband goodnight, I sat in the living room to unwind after a long day. I hate it when men say, "Homemakers just have to stay at home and play with the kids all day." They have no idea how overwhelming it can be.

Anyway, I didn't want to sit outside. It only depresses me wondering how you're doing without me. Laughing is hard these days. I have a good marriage and the kids are well behaved for the most part. Life couldn't be grander.

It dawned on me as I turned off the TV and sat in the silence, my husband doesn't know you at all. He's a workaholic and you like to stay at home. There's no wonder I

74

feel empty. You and I were inseparable at one time and now I spend my evenings alone. The quietness is nice, but it doesn't fill the void.

I hope you're doing well and are happy. Can you at least let me know that you're alive? A sister needs to know.

I await your response,

Rebecca

Dear friend, Rich,

It's been a long week, between work and worrying about you. It made my day when I got home and found a letter from you in my mailbox. I rushed in the house and ripped open the envelope as I plopped down on my couch. With heart pounding anticipation, I began reading, not sure what you wanted to say to me.

It's good to hear you made a friend there. I'd like to hear more about him. It sounds like you met him in this tavern. Not to jump to conclusions, but apparently you two drink together. That concerns me. I'm aware of your past, as you know, so I've asked the Lord's help in this matter.

There is a God who loves you very much. Telling yourself He doesn't care about you is the real lie. Prayer is a powerful tool He wants us to freely exercise. The anger you hold onto will remain there until you give it to God. You can't bury the pain. It will keep creeping up on you.

The margaritas may make you feel good for a short time, but what happens when the glass is empty? You order another one…then another. Eventually you're staggering or worse. Then you wake up the next day with a hangover and the pain from your past is still there.

Think about the money you're spending on alcohol and the damage you're doing to your body. You don't need me to lecture you on the effects of drinking on a regular basis. I will say you are worth more than that. Freedom is your choice.

I can assure you God isn't mad at you and He surely doesn't hate you. That's silly talk from a person who has been hurt a lot. I understand where you're coming from. Rehab was the most trying time in my life and I never want to go back down that road again.

To answer your question about who is praying for you: your family as well as me. I also added you to the prayer chain at church. No, I didn't use your name. I asked that everyone pray for a

FORGIVENESS IS A CHOICE

close friend of mine who doesn't know the Lord.

I laughed at your comment about becoming an Eskimo and selling ice. I needed a good laugh as I deal with all this. That sense of humor is what I miss the most about you. It would be good to hear your voice again, but I know you don't want that. I won't push the envelope.

If you don't want to contact your mother, I can't make you. How about saying hi to your sister, Rebecca. I believe she's authentic when she says she misses her brother. Harsh words would be better than nothing at all.

What did you mean by, you "needed to look at this retreat objectively?" I worried you moved again and I wouldn't hear from you anymore. Now I learn you spent the whole time getting drunk with some old man. I'm sorry, but I don't find that "objective."

You know I only say these things out of love. You can thank Jesus for that, He's the author of love. He demonstrated it when He hung on the cross. Consider picking up

your Bible and getting into a good
church.

Write soon,

Kelly

Rebecca,

I'm only writing you because I'm drunk. It takes 6 margaritas to persuade me to waste my time. I staggered up my stairs and fell into my living room, but for some reason I couldn't sleep. It's probably because of all the hounding letters.

I'm not sure what you want me to say after all this time. I came here to be alone and get away from you idiots. This may sound rhetorical, but what do you want? You tried to get me locked away in a funny farm and it steams you that it didn't work.

Well, guess what? I still drink and probably more heavily thanks to you and the rest of your family where I never belonged. I'm glad you had a place to call home. Some of us weren't that lucky or maybe I deserve to be kicked aside and put out with the trash. I know that mother of yours feels that way. Don't try to dispute me. I know she didn't want me. It's obvious.

It was a mistake to write you. I'm just getting mad all over again. You all pushed me away, so congratulations…you won.

Have a nice life without me,

Angry Rich

Kelly,

Well, I did it. I wrote my youngest sister. It wasn't easy, nor did I have anything nice to say. She asked for it, so she got what she deserved. I was smashed and needed to drink more after talking to that back stabber.

Since you figured out I have a drinking buddy, we can talk about it. He's been a good influence and gives me lots of wisdom. The tavern is a great place to unwind and watch a ball game. It's the only place I can laugh.

I'm glad you have a faith in god, whatever that means. Everyone needs something to believe in, so enjoy. That's just not for me. He may love you. You're worth loving. I'm not. I'm better off where I am, away from human contact. It's the greatest feeling in the world to be free.

I don't need your "god" to free me from anything, so you can tell everyone to stop the prayers. That's the most ridiculous thing I've ever heard. I hope you realize you're talking to the air when you pray. There's no one there.

If there really is a god out there, he wouldn't have put me with a family who rejected me. How do you expect me to believe in a supreme being who is all powerful? That's just nonsense.

I'm sorry for sounding so harsh. Hearing from you always makes me smile. I wish you would stop bringing up your god though. The concept of believing in something impossible to prove doesn't fall into the common-sense category. I don't care how many Bible verses you bring up or churches you visit. There's nothing that will convince me to associate with a bunch of shirt and ties who show up on Sunday with a fake smile.

I think my quiet time without writing you was good for me. You may think it was all about drinking all the time, but that's from sticking your nose in that Bible. It has corrupted the most intelligent people in the world. Those scriptures are so vague the most educated scholars can't agree on what they mean.

I'd hate to think you are judging me. Doesn't your religion say not to judge people? I use margaritas as a tool, just as a boxer uses gloves to be productive.

I'm always under time constraints in my job. I know I work at home, but my projects always take more time than I can do them in. I'm always telling my managers it's not humanly possible to complete the work in 40 hours. So, I have no choice but to put in 70 or 80 hours a week to keep up. It's great that I make good money and can do it without bosses and co-workers looking over my shoulder.

I'm sure you don't appreciate a word of what I've said, but it's the way I feel. I think it's more important to tell the truth than to pretend to be perfect.

That's it for now. Have a good night,

Rich

Dear brother Rich,

The anxiety rose in me when I saw you finally responded to me. I let the letter sit on my kitchen table as I sipped coffee on this quiet Saturday afternoon. When I finally opened it, I was shocked to see how angry you still are. Every part of me knew you were going to be unpleasant, but I never dreamed it would be so harsh.

I suppose you think I'm horrible for calling the ambulance that night, but I didn't know what else to do. You were passed out...unresponsive. Think about what you would've done if the roles were reversed. It's not in your nature to let someone die, and it looked like you were taking your last breath.

I'm tearing up as I think about all this again. That nightmare followed me for several weeks, long after you left for Washington.

I can't tell you how many times I woke in the middle of the night, wondering how you were doing way up there. I didn't even know where you went, just like the rest of the family. We didn't have a clue what happened to you.

I know you think you were deserted and have no one who loves you, but Rich, that couldn't be further from the truth. Families argue and fight from time to time, but that doesn't mean they hate each other. The feud between us needs to stop.

The problems you have with mom should be kept between you and her. I'm sorry she hurt you. I can't answer for her decision to give you away. Believe me, no one thinks you're garbage, including mom. Don't tell yourself that.

85

Try to consider that she took you in when we were small so we all could get to know you and spend time with you. Everyone liked having you around, especially mom. When the weekend was over, she used to cry as your foster parents came to get you.

Try not to be so mad at me, I really love you and miss you dearly. Thank you for writing me back.

I hope to hear from you soon,

Rebecca

Hard working Rich,

Thanks for being honest. No, I don't want you to put up a front. Being yourself is what I admire about you. However, I talk about God because He's the center of my universe. He created me and has a plan for my life. I don't bring it up to insult you, only to show you what He's done for me and help you understand He can do it for you too.

I can tell you I'm not talking to the air when I pray. I hear what you're saying and understand your frustration. The fact is, not all church goers are bad people. I go to church and I would never judge you. I am, however, extremely concerned for you. That's why I pray for you, as others do.

I'm glad you decided to write to your sister. I know it brightened her day. It's a big step for you to contact her. It doesn't matter that you weren't nice to her. She needs to know you are safe and alive. I'd like to hear more about your interactions with her. Don't stop writing.

FORGIVENESS IS A CHOICE

I can attest to the alcohol thing.
I know how it feels to medicate
your pain. Whoever this friend
is, I can't say he's a good
influence on you. I know reading
this will make you mad, but I have
to say it. Drinking isn't the
answer.

It's good that you can laugh and I
know how much you love sports.
The combination of the two must
lift your spirits to the clouds.
There's nothing wrong with having
a good time. Even Christians need
to laugh and enjoy a good evening.

It sounds like you're doing well
with your career. I originally
was concerned that you wouldn't
find a decent job after leaving
your prestigious position in
Kansas City. Apparently, working
from home is a perfect match for
you. Too bad you have to put in
such long hours, but it makes the
days go by faster.

I have refrained from talking
about my feelings in all of this.
I try to focus on your needs. I
can't keep quiet anymore. I've
mentioned your family needs you
and miss you. The fact of the

LETTERS FROM SECLUSION

matter is, I miss you too. It
would be good to hear your voice
and see you again.

I didn't save you from that
horrible accident to never see you
again,

Your Best Friend Kelly

My Mentor,

It's good to see you after the night I had last night. It was a little embarrassing falling in the parking lot. I didn't think I had that much to drink. Many people passed me by and said stupid things, but didn't lift a finger to help. That's the way of the world, everyone cares for themselves.

I'm glad you came to my aid. It shows I'm not just a drinking buddy to you. My knees and right hip hurts really bad today. I almost went to the doctor, but all that office wants is money, not to see me become well. Why should I line their pockets any more than necessary?

I've come to the conclusion that writing to Kelly and Rebecca is causing me more pain. I can't take it. Neither one understands me. I told them I come here and am able to laugh and they try to tell me you're not good for me. How should they know? They just hate it that I moved away. I will live my life my way, just as they do things as they choose.

I get sick of all these Bible thumpers judging me. Neither one can get past the idea of my having a few drinks after work. In their minds, that makes me an alcoholic who's going straight to hell. I don't have time for that nonsense.

I don't mean to start the evening complaining, but it gets under my skin,

Rich

Young Fella,

You can vent whenever you want to. If you can't bring your problems to good friends, who can you talk to? I'm here every night, as you know. So, go ahead...let's talk.

As much as I hate to admit it, you crack me up sometimes. I'm not saying your problems don't matter, it's just that I can remember being your age and saying the same things. I learned the things you're experiencing now. Good folks just aren't out there.

I have to say, picking you up off the ground isn't something I can do every day. These old bones aren't made for that garbage. I had to help my only friend, since, like you say, no one else was going to. Do me a favor and try to stay on your feet from now on...I don't need a hernia. It sucks getting old.

There's no point in talking about your friends and family again and again. They are who they are. You can't change them. Look at it this way: If you want them to accept you, you have to accept them with all their annoying traits. It may be best not to talk to them all the time.

I agree, this talk about the Bible is a bunch of bologna. Some really smart, but deranged man, wrote that as fact and people believed every word of it. I choose to laugh at the stupidity of people. It's better than getting annoyed. There are so many religious writings out there. Who knows which one is right...any? I'm sure they all are someone's idea of what might be true. I really think it's all fantasy.

It doesn't take a whole lot of common sense to see no one can raise a staff and part the Red Sea. How about that Jesus guy who changed water into wine? If only that was possible, I could run wine through my kitchen sink. That would be nice. This bar would go out of business. Noah's Ark couldn't possibly be true, either. How can anyone fit every species of animal on one boat? I don't care how big it was, the weight alone would sink it. What a laugh!

I could go on, but there's no sense. It's just fun to pick at Christians about their beliefs. Many have gone into a church, thinking they would come out with a better life. I hate to tell them the world won't change because they "accepted the Lord." It's a crutch weak people use to handle life's pressures.

You can believe what you want. I really don't care. I just don't have time to waste on that garbage. While all the Christians are going to church, I'm sleeping in my comfortable bed until I choose to get up.

Now that I got a good laugh, let's talk about something worthwhile...Sheila. I noticed her looking at you again. It's not just to see if you need another drink. I know that's what you think, but I think she's trying to get your attention.

We've talked about pushing the world away, but when a beauty like that comes along, it's hard to say no.

I have a suspicion she's available. Why else would she check you out? If I were you, I would forget my past and talk to her. You don't have to ask her out right away, just say hi and watch how she responds. I'll bet she's dying for you to make the first move.

Don't be a chicken...go for it,

Your encouraging Mentor

Old but wise Mentor,

I'd like to talk about your comments on religion, accepting my family and only friend from Kansas City. However, it's not important now. I appreciate that you agree and support me in all of it, but Sheila just smiled at me.

My heart is pounding. I think you're right. She keeps looking my way for no reason. I want to talk to her so bad. I need another drink to calm my nerves. The only problem is I have to order it from her. I guess there's no way out.

Twenty minutes have gone by and I haven't made a move. You keep nudging me and calling me a coward. I'm used to being alone where no one can bother me. Now I want some female company. It feels weird.

My heart is pounding harder as I anticipate approaching her. I'm going to do it. As I get up taking a deep breath, I pretend to be calm. There's a guy at the bar talking to her now. He's real buff with flowing blonde hair. She won't bother with me when she can have a nice physique like his. I'll just order another drink and leave it be.

She's laughing as I rest my elbows on the bar with one foot propped on the footrest. I'd like to think she was paying attention to me. It's not the case.

This stocky guy has her laughing and having a good time. I don't know what to say or if I should say anything. It's not polite to interfere.

Lost in the effort,

Rich

Young Chicken Rich,

Stop making excuses. Why did you come back to the table like Sheila is just another server? So what if she's talking to another man? He's just a customer. She needs to play nice to him, that's how she makes the big tips. Use your head and stop feeling sorry for yourself.

Let me take a step back. I don't want to pressure you. I want to say take your time and wait until you feel comfortable, but I know you...you'll never do it. If I was a young fellow, I'd jump on it.

This may come to a surprise to you, but she peered at you when you left the bar and came back to our table. I'm sure you noticed it didn't take long for her to bring over another round of alcohol.

I'm glad you think I'm supportive. That's why I'm here. You're not just a drinking buddy who happens to like the same baseball and football teams. It makes it easier to chat with someone who's younger and been through the same stuff, but there's more to you than that.

I'm glad we met. You make life interesting again. Since you started coming into the tavern, the crowds have picked up during the ballgames. They love to watch your reactions. I don't know what's worse, when you hop and cheer when things go well or the way you get hostile when they don't. You're hilarious.

I think I'll hang around a while tonight. Something tells me it may get interesting in here, since it's a Saturday night.

Minding my own business,

Your mentor

Mentor,

I'm taking a deep breath as I drink down the last of my margarita. Just as I expected, it calmed my nerves. Sheila is so beautiful and friendly…oh boy…I wish I could find the words to start a conversation.

I suppose I have nothing to lose. The worst she can do is reject me like everyone else. I'm drunk enough to have the nerve. At least, if she says no, it won't hurt as much.

Don't think you're pushing me too much. I need you to lead me in the right direction. The idea of having a relationship after all I've been through is so foreign. My biggest fear, I guess, isn't about rejection at all. There's only a slim chance I will learn to trust her.

With all the hounding letters from my family and friend, I don't need any more drama in my life. This isn't a good time to pursue her. No…I won't do it.

Let's talk about something else.

I noticed more people come in when sports are on TV. I thought that was normal for the bar scene.

Wait a minute…I see her out of the corner of my eye. Sheila is smiling at me…or is she looking in my direction, but at someone else? It's hard to tell. I don't want to make a fool of myself by looking at her again. She'll know for sure I'm interested.

I'm clueless,

Rich

Pathetic Rich,

What's wrong with you? Good grief! You keep making excuses and asking me questions I can't answer. Go over to the bar and talk to Sheila.

Stop purposely looking away from her. If you wait too long, someone else will put the moves on her. You know she's pretty and friendly, so get off your duff.

This isn't about your mother or sisters or Kelly. They should matter, but not right now. Forget about them and don't let your baggage get in the way. Don't get on my nerves, you young twerp.

See, here she comes again...but she's going to a different table nearby. She sat down to talk to her customers. The last hour is always the busiest here. Yes, I said the **last** hour. That means if you don't act soon, another day will go by.

I have to laugh at you...again. I don't think I've met to guy who's so shy. I remember being shy at a young age, meaning my teenage years and maybe my early twenties, but you're not that young anymore. How long is it gonna take you to man up? You waiting for Medicare?

Getting older by the minute,

Mentor

Sheila,

I thought I'd catch you for another margarita before you make it back behind the bar. I saw you talking to those guys at the next table. You like to talk and flirt. I'm assuming they flirted back. It's too loud in here to hear what you all were talking about…not that it's any of my business.

I'll let you make your final rounds before closing. Hopefully, I'll see you in a few minutes. The longer these people in here drink, the louder they become. It's near deafening sometimes.

Watching as you walk away,

Rich

Wise Mentor,

Well I did it. I talked to her a little. You sure were quiet when she was here. Maybe I should think you're as shy as me. Perhaps you wanted to step out of the way, to allow me to have her undivided attention. Either way, my heart was pounding so fast...I can't describe it.

I still don't know if she's interested in me. Of course, it's too soon to tell. Let me take a deep breath and slurp the last few drops left in my glass. I need all the alcohol I can get. What is it about women that makes us act like this?

Actually, I have a better question? What if she ends up like all the other women I've met? People say, a man falls for a woman who is like their mother. That's the last thing I need.

I'm thinking I should stick to my guns and forget this whole thing. I don't need another back-stabbing female. I see you shaking your head at me, but it doesn't matter. You're the one who told me not to trust anyone.

That's it...I'm done. We both will be better off if we just hang out here and forget about others.

Wait...Sheila is bringing my drink. She touched my back as she slapped it on the table. It's been a long time since I felt dainty fingers. It's

FORGIVENESS IS A CHOICE

uncomfortable and soothing at the same time. I wonder if she touches all the guys who come in here.

She sat down between us. What should I say?

Nervous and playing it cool,

Rich

Handsome Rich,

I've never gotten a chance to talk to you. I see you're quiet and a little shy. It's no secret. I think it's cute.

I'm sure you've noticed a lot of the same people in here every night. I've been doing this for 5 years and I can tell you nothing changes. The women are here to unwind and get away from their husbands and male bosses. At least 5 of them are here right now.

All of them say men are idiots who can't think for themselves. The men think women are emotional imbeciles. Everybody thinks they belong to the superior gender.

It's a never-ending battle of the sexes. Women badmouth the men and the men put down the women. I roll my eyes at them all. It's a shallow way of going through life assuming all men and all women are the same. What a boring world we would be in if that were true.

A lot of the men I talk to in here think it's okay to put their hands on me just because they're drunk. I have to play along so they will tip me.

I'm sure you've figured that out. Just because you're quiet, doesn't mean you're dumb.

That's why I decided to stop by before closing. It's a cinch to see you're not the aggressive type. I love you're smile and dark brown eyes. As I touch your hand, I can feel you tremble. Apparently, it's been a while since you've been in a relationship.

You don't have to talk about that if you don't want. That's okay. I'm more interested to learn about you. Where are you from? What makes you come in here every night?

You don't seem like the bar type.

Sheila

Mentor,

For the first time, you don't offer any insight or wisdom for me. Sheila not only came to the table, but she sat between us and started talking to me. She's even more beautiful close up. It furthers my nervousness.

I'm so afraid I will say the wrong thing and make her think I'm unintelligent. I peered at you a few times as a hint. If you say something it will lessen the tension. Now it feels like my mentor has turned into a statue.

What should I say to her?

Rich

Sheila,

I don't mean to be so hesitant. I apologize. This is a good environment for me after a long day at work. These clients of mine are worse than my demanding boss. If I wasn't able to work at home, I would seek work elsewhere.

I'm flattered you took time out to start a conversation with me. At first, I came in here to unwind and check out the place. Then I found you. I guess it won't hurt to tell you how strikingly beautiful you are. I'm fidgeting as I talk to you. I guess I'm not very good at hiding my feelings.

This old guy who sits next to me has been a good influence. We talk about lots of personal things I thought I would never discuss with anyone. Even though our ages are miles apart, we're not that different.

I see you're not interested in talking about him. You didn't even glance over at him. Instead, you started rubbing your fingers over my hand. I'm guessing you don't do that for every customer. Maybe I should order another margarita before closing.

You've asked me a couple questions about myself. I've been avoiding them or not answering fully.

My past isn't pleasant… Excuse me while I take a drink. Sorry, I gulped. Anyway, I've been through a lot so I'm hoping you don't ask too much.

The things I'm saying may be a big turn off, but it's the truth. You're still smiling. That's a good sign, I suppose. How about that last margarita? The bar hasn't closed yet.

Fumbling for words to say,

Rich

Stammering Rich,

You really need to relax. No, the bar isn't closed yet, but I think you've had enough. As I listen to you talk, it's clear to me how open you are. Integrity goes a long way and my intuition tells me you're a nice guy.

I'm glad you have a friend who is supportive. We all need that. My girlfriends are fun to be around, but most of them moved on to other areas of the country and overseas. It's funny how time changes the world around us.

Tell me more about what you do for a living. You already know what I do. It's nothing glamorous, but it pays the bills. Not to brag, but I make the highest tips of all the bartenders here. It's hard work and fun at the same time.

You don't have to leave a big tip tonight. I would much rather meet you after closing, even if it's just a walk under the street lamps. I know it's late, but I like quiet things after a noisy shift.

My boss looked over at me and gave me a hard look. He likes to give me a hard time when he sees me hanging out with customers, but it's how I make the tips. It's getting busy again. All the last minute drink orders are coming in. No one thinks they're drunk enough. They have to top it off with a side of loudness.

I hope to see you after work,

Sheila

Shy Rich,

I told you she was digging on you. Too bad she had to make the first move, but hey...at least you're getting somewhere with her now. All the wasted time you spent wondering what might have happened is over.

In your defense, I understand not wanting to get rejected again. I have more years of that under my belt than anything else. I don't even want to think about how long it went on and by how many people. It makes me mad all over again. Maybe I need to join the crowd of last minute drink. So what if it comes with a side of stupid...or whatever Sheila said.

You looking over at me when she first came over here makes you look like you can't think for yourself. I don't mean to be rude, but I wasn't about to get into your conversation, when Sheila obviously showed an interest in you...not me. You did just fine, even though you were shaking like an epileptic.

I guess I'll call it a night. You have a date tonight, as soon as all the drunks find a home. Hanging around with you makes me stick around much later than I used to. I'm getting too old for this.

Sleepy beyond belief,

Mentor

Cop-Out Mentor,

Go ahead and leave me here alone. See if I care. I was wondering if Sheila wouldn't mind seeing me tomorrow before she comes to work. I have another busy day tomorrow.

Although, I'm curious to see what she's really after. Women always have a motive. It may be nothing to worry about, but I need to keep up my guard.

The anxiety is rising as I think about the endless possibilities. What if she treats me nice for a while, then gets tired of me and starts putting me down? I would have, once again, wasted my time on another relationship.

I like my privacy. It's the only thing that gives me peace. If I let another female interrupt that, it will destroy me all over again. Oh boy…I don't know what to do.

You've gotten up and left me now. So, I guess you don't have anything to add to what you've already told me. No one likes talking to themselves.

Preparing for my date,

Rich

Brown-Eyed Rich,

I never thought I was going to get out of there. Anticipating seeing you made the last hour drag on for weeks, it seemed. I appreciate you waiting for me. I know it's late.

My work week ends tonight, so I have a couple days off. Judging from my line of work, you probably think I have a wild life. Actually, I like relaxing in a quiet environment. It helps combat the rambunctious bar scene.

I have a roommate who likes to party. She's a college student. I shake my head or roll my eyes at her most of the time, but I shouldn't be critical. There was a time when I was a crazy teenager, glad to be out of my parents clutches. If you want to hear about my wild days, we can both get a good laugh.

Enough about me. It's time to shut up and let you talk. I know you don't want to talk about your past, but a girl needs to know, at least, a little about you. Don't worry, I've been out with all the bad boys. There can't be anything you've done that can top some of these losers I've dated.

This time of night is so peaceful. I always walk home because it's the only quiet time I have. Sometimes I wish I could afford to live alone. It would help my sanity...at least for a while. Oh, well. A bartender only makes so much.

So, I'm curious what made you chose this little town. Understandably, it's not far from Everett, where I grew up. I like it here, in Maple Falls, because it's away from the big city and still close enough to visit family. I make the hour and a half drive once a month and stay with my father overnight.

My family became distant after my parents' divorce. Even after my mother's death 3 years ago, my siblings and cousins don't keep in touch. If it wasn't for my father, I wouldn't see them at all.

I must admit, I've always been a daddy's girl. That's why men don't stick around. I don't know why guys are threatened by a woman's relationship with her father. I hope you can explain it.

I know I sound like a bitter, middle aged woman, but I'm really not. I just want to be completely transparent. As I've said, that's an important trait to me.

I said I was going to let you talk, but I keep beating my gums. You still seem nervous. Please relax and tell me about you.

What do you do for a living? Have you ever been married? Kids?

I'll let you talk now,

Sheila

Smiling Sheila,

I think I've learned your whole life story in the first 10 minutes of our midnight walk. What else is there to talk about under the bright stars? You've had some disappointments in life, by what I'm hearing.

Unlike yourself, I have no interest in seeing my family. To say I came from a broken home wouldn't even come close to reality. We could talk all night about my many foster homes and families, but I'm really not interested. I'm eager to get to know you and what you're looking for in a relationship.

To be completely frank, I was hesitant to get involved with another woman or even another friend. I'm shy, as you know, and enjoy my privacy. I live about 20 minutes away from here, in Glacier. I purposely chose a house that was secluded, away from other people.

With all that said, I chose to meet with you. It's a gamble, but I think you're worth it. It's not every day a young beautiful woman gives me positive attention. It's a refreshing change.

Speaking of "young" woman, you mentioned you were middle aged. There's no way you're in your forties. I assume that's what you mean by "middle aged." You appear to be in your twenties…maybe early thirties. I could pick you out of the crowded bar room by your black hair and brown eyes. Even if you weren't tending bar, I would have noticed.

I'm a computer software engineer and have been doing it for over 20 years. I come from big city too and made a lot more money before I decided to move here. It's high pressure, but I make extremely good money. It's worth the hassle.

Unfortunately, I don't have any days off. When this company hired me, I was told the work load was heavy, but I never dreamed I would be so overworked. I feel like I'm getting too old for this already. I'm hoping to retire early, so I keep that in mind when I feel like pulling my hair out.

I've never been married and have no kids. That is one thing I'm proud to say, which says a lot. I've done some things I can't exactly brag about. I came here looking for peace and I found it. Now it's just a matter of finding who I really am.

I have really enjoyed being here. I've never had so much fun. The first year was hard, but I adapted. I had no choice in my line of work. There's a high demand for people who can design software, although that's only part of what I do. I won't bore you with the details.

I'm sorry to hear about your mother. It sounds like you had a strained relationship with her and your extended family. Everyone has their baggage. Perhaps we can trade stories.

It won't be tonight. It's late and I've walked you to your door. I don't hear partying going on inside, so you have more quiet time than you thought.

I hope to see you again,

Content Rich

Little Brother,

I figured you would ignore my last letter. It doesn't matter, we still love you and pray for you all the time. I'm hoping you took the time to work through the anger and try to understand that I came to your aid, not to ruin your life.

To take my mind off our dysfunctional family, I rearranged the furniture in my house. The living room looked great. I moved the couch next to the bay window that overlooks the front lawn and porch, just as it was in mom's house. I think she still keeps it that way.

As I sat in my easy chair to take a rest, I couldn't help but look out at the dusk sky. Kansas City is rather congested and industrial. The day turned to a peaceful night. It's amazing how magical the darkness can be.

FORGIVENESS IS A CHOICE

I tried to control my emotions, but the nighttime means stars; stars mean constellations. It was like a gust of wind forced me outside. Orion was there in the center of the sky, it seemed. He stared at me while I wept.

I waited a while to make sure my family was asleep before I headed into the basement. I almost forgot about all the star charts and notes we made. They were hidden in a box under a broken table. I keep them there so my husband doesn't find them. He thinks I worry about you too much.

After dusting off the box and rummaging through it, I came across one chart that featured Orion. It was loaded with your handwriting, explaining the significance of the constellation and how it linked with the other constellations around it. To say it was bittersweet would be an understatement.

Everything around me reminds me of you. We have so many good memories, but unfortunately, they lead to hurt feelings now. I wish it wasn't this way, but I have no idea how to fix it. A relationship has to go two ways.

Now I'm going to ask you to forgive me. It may seem impossible and I'm trying to understand how you feel.

I hope you will open your heart,

Rebecca

Old Mentor,

You may be old, but you're a lot sharper than I thought. Last night was awesome. Sheila and I talked as I walked her home. It's weird that she wanted to hang out with me. There are so many guys in that bar every night who are a lot better looking and younger than me. It makes me wonder why she singled me out.

Whatever the reason, it was nice to have some positive female attention. Much to my surprise, she has a strained relationship with her family as well. She didn't go into detail, but it didn't take her long to open up and talk about it.

I wish I could say the same on my part. I still don't know what she's after. As much as I'd like to think her intentions are pure, I don't want to get burned again. What if she's after my money? The first question she asked me was about my line of work.

Going home last night felt altogether different. For the first time since I moved into that house, I felt lonely. I lay staring through my bedroom window, trying to fall asleep. There's nothing to see through any of my windows but a bunch of trees. I can't even see the sky at night. During the day, not much light comes in.

What am I complaining about? That's exactly what I wanted. My house is perfect for me. No one can bother me and try to take advantage of me. It just felt empty for the first time.

Things will be different tonight without Sheila. She's off and enjoying a couple days with her family in Everett. There are a couple of guys at the bar getting drunk before the sun set. It will be another eventful evening. What do I care? After another stressful day at work, I'll accept anything that doesn't put me in the grave.

Here's to another round,

Rich

Relaxed Rich,

You sure have gained some confidence since you left here last night. Something tells me you did more than walk her home. I won't jump to conclusions, but since you're on the subject of my experience in life, I'll say I sense an event you don't want to discuss. That's your choice.

You noticed the two drunks at the bar. What about the girls that just walked in and sat on the opposite side, near the jukebox. They didn't sit there for no reason. Why not talk to them and keep your options open? As the saying goes, there's more than one way to swing a bat.

The game will be on soon, so I'll go grab another beer and you a margarita. I may tell the bartender to double-up on your tequila. Why not cut to the chase and get drunk early tonight. It's good the cops are never out. You would've been charged with 15 DUI's by now.

Relax and live it up,

Mentor

Know-It-All Mentor,

Think whatever you want. I don't care. I appreciate you grabbing me a margarita, but that doesn't give you the right to accuse me of sleeping with Sheila. I've always been honest with you. Trust me, if I spent the night with her, I would have the bragging rights and tell you as soon as I could.

It was the longest walk in history. We discussed so much. Getting to know a person is next to impossible. It's especially hard when I keep my guard up in fear of what's going on inside her.

I've noticed how everything looks so different after dark. This is a peaceful town anyway, but at night, the world smiles. The sunshine makes everyone angry. At least, that's how I see it. My time of day is the dark time.

I don't know about approaching two strange girls, just because they came in without guys. Maybe they want to get away from men and have a good laugh. They are good-looking, and one keeps staring at me. I wonder what they're saying about me.

Enough about them. I have something serious to talk about. My sister, Rebecca, wrote me again. It's a good thing you got me this potent margarita.

I may need a few more. She keeps trying to push our past relationship down my throat. I don't care that we had fun looking at the stars and studying the constellations. That's done and over with. It doesn't give her the right to get me thrown in a hospital for crazy people. She's crazy if she thinks writing me a letter is supposed to make me forget about it.

What is it going to take to make those clowns leave me alone? Apparently ignoring them isn't giving them a hint to go away. I knew writing her that nasty letter was a mistake. It's like feeding cats, one nibble and they'll bug you forever. The thing that really irks me is, she's telling me everyone is praying for me.

I'm going to guzzle this last bit of my drink and get another...or two,

Disgusted Rich

Rich,

Once again, I have to shake my head at you. This thing about your sister, I get. You don't have to talk to her again if you don't want, but you should tell her to get lost. Your family reminds me of mine. No one cares about anyone, so they really need to stop pretending.

Naturally she said everyone is praying. That's what people say when you don't do what they want. Don't let anyone bully or manipulate you. You're a nice guy. You don't deserve that junk.

If you're dead set on not mingling with other women, it's fine with me. I don't want you to waste time with one woman if she ends up taking advantage of you, then dumps you. That's why I said, "Keep your options open." Life is a chess game. Every move you make will affect your end game. I just think the two girls are cute, and yes, the brunette is checking you out.

I miss the days when I went out with a different girl every night. That's no exaggeration. I was a ladies man in my

FORGIVENESS IS A CHOICE

day. The only good memories I have are of all the chicks. Oh well, that's a time I will never see again. So, go for it while you're still young enough.

I'm glad you and Sheila had a nice time together. Your hormones are all worked up. Don't forget, it's exciting in the beginning. Give it a few months, if it lasts that long, and see how you feel about each other. It's a slow fade that everyone goes through.

Watch what you're doing there. Getting another drink doesn't require a grand entrance. There you go again, tripping and falling. Good luck getting the bartender to serve you.

Laughing,

Mentor

Mentor,

If I wasn't so drunk, I would be embarrassed. I didn't know my foot was caught under my chair. I can still function just fine. I'll make it to the bar okay. Some people are staring, but at least they're laughing. I can't help it if I'm a klutz.

Now I need to convince the bartender to serve me. I don't know this guy, so I can't use my friendship to get my way. Some people make a big deal about little things. It was only a chair I knocked over. It's not like I damaged anything.

Oh boy! I'm in luck. Sheila came in. I thought she was in Everett with her family. Whatever...she can get me a drink now.

Don't laugh at me, old man. You've fallen down a few times too. Just because I didn't see you, doesn't mean you haven't. Don't act so innocent.

Ignoring you,

Rich

Drunk Rich,

It's a good thing I came in when I did. I thought I'd come home early and surprise you. Good grief, Rich, what's wrong with you? You don't need any more alcohol. Let me help you up.

Now that you're in a chair, tell me what made you drink so much. You don't fall down when I'm working. I don't mean to give you the third degree, but we just started dating. A girl needs to know that her man isn't an alcoholic. I've had such bad luck with men.

Sorry to jump down your throat. I left my family after only a few hours. It wasn't a pleasant visit. My brother and sister came over to dad's house about an hour after I arrived. I was having a quiet talk with my father before they got there. I wish it stayed that way.

I didn't know they were planning on coming over. Sometimes they do, but most of the time I don't see them. I love my siblings, but after about 10 minutes, I'm ready for them to be somewhere else. If you only knew what I've been through with them. I can't stand the way they nitpick me. Being older doesn't give them the right to judge everything I do.

I feel bad that I left my dad. We were laughing and tossing old stories. He loves to talk about the things I did when I was a little girl. I keep reminding him I'm an adult now, but it's still funny to hear him talk about it. He used to call me his "little princess." He still does on occasion.

It all got interrupted by my knucklehead siblings, who came in and didn't even say hello to me. My sister, Sabrina, hugged dad and said, "I didn't want you to be alone with her," referring to me. He shook his head and said, "Why don't you greet your sister? You don't get to see her much." It didn't matter, Sabrina and my brother, Sebastian, both ignored my presence.

I rolled my eyes and continued to talk to dad. I didn't care that they were there. He defended me, which is rare. He keeps his mouth shut most of the time. I guess it's easier that way.

We all went to Romano's for lunch. Dad insisted on buying. While we were waiting for our food, I ignored Sabrina and Sebastian, just as they were ignoring me, and started asking dad questions about his health. He's older and will eventually need care.

I saw Sabrina whisper something to Sebastian. Dad let out a sigh and said, "You don't have to worry about me yet. I'm doing fine." Sabrina slapped her hand on the table and scoffed. I finally had enough and said, "What is your problem?"

Sabrina looked around the table, as to expect someone to back her up. "You know, you don't have to be so rude to me." That's when the feud started. Dad raised his arm to try to calm everyone down, but I waited too long to tell off my brother and sister.

I won't repeat what I said, but I can tell you it wasn't nice. The restaurant got quiet and people peered at us. Both my siblings tried to tell me I was being childish and if I really cared about my family, I wouldn't have moved away. That's when I left. There was no point in talking about it and disturbing other people's lunch. I told dad I was sorry, but I couldn't stay any longer.

Is any of this making sense to you or are you so drunk you don't care? I see you looking down. The table can't be that interesting. I really need your input.

Looking for support,

Sheila

Distressed Sheila,

I'm listening to everything you're saying. It's hard to hear all this and not get angry. No one needs to be treated that way. You shouldn't tolerate that from those two clowns. I know they're your only siblings, but forget about them. Stay away from those who purposely hurt you.

Don't believe the things they say. You are far from selfish. If they didn't like you moving, they should have treated you better and maybe you would have stayed. I'm sure they never thought of that. It's not like you moved 2000 miles away. You're only 90 or so miles from there. How narcissistic can they be?

I know all about family members who don't care about you. I grew up with that. I don't want to turn this into a conversation about me, so I won't say any more about it.

It takes a cold-hearted person to put you down in the middle of a restaurant. It seems they wanted to go there just to belittle you in front of a bunch of people.

Sorry that happened to you. It makes me mad. You're a nice person and don't deserve that.

Why don't you have a drink? I'm buying this round for you, this old guy next to you, and me.

Order what you want. Let someone serve you for a change. You deserve a treat.

My blood pressure is rising,

Rich

Supportive Rich,

Thanks for finally speaking up. I was thinking you didn't care. The temptation to get drunk with you right now is overwhelming, but I think I'll pass. You can barely function as it is. I don't mean to be rude to your friend, but I'd rather get out of here and into someplace quiet.

Much to my surprise, you stood on your own. I still don't think you should drive. I'll help you to the door. Don't be stubborn, I don't want you to fall. Geesh...men!

Now that we're outside, can I take you home? Don't go near your car. You're not driving tonight. Your friend, the one you call old guy, agrees with me. This is the last thing I need right now.

Exasperated,

Shiela

Nagging Sheila,

I'm trying not to get upset. You're starting
to sound like my mother. She never stops
trying to control me. I hope you're not that
kind of girl. You sure are beautiful and I'd
like to keep you around. I'll do what you
want, but stop nagging.

Your sister doesn't know the definition of
moving away. I moved 2000 miles away
from my hometown. I did it purposely to
get my mother and sisters out of my life, and
I will never regret it.

Some people walk through life with regret
and miss out on their joy. I'm not going to
be one of those people.

Why are you holding me like a baby? I can
walk. If you don't want me to drive, I
won't. Let's go somewhere away from
other people. That's the way we both like it.

Don't get me wrong. It feels good to have
you hold me, but do it because you want to
touch me rather than because you think I
need taking care of. I'll humor you and let

you help me into your car, since you won't let me drive mine.

The seats in your car feel great. I put my head back and the world started spinning. I hate to admit it, but you're right, I am drunk. Maybe I should rest here for a while.

Thanks for reclining my seat,

Dizzy Rich

Rich,

Even when you're inebriated, you're still cute. I love watching you lay back in the passenger's seat with your eyes closed. I'm picky about who I will go out with. Despite the circumstances, I think I made a good choice.

Sorry I jumped on you when I came into the tavern. I wanted to surprise you with a visit and I was hoping we could spend some time together while I'm off. It shocked me when I saw you fall down. I hope you don't do that again. Don't think I believe it's the first time. I've been watching you.

Since you're not responding to what I'm saying, other than an occasional nod, I'll let you rest. I hope you don't wake with a backache. These seats aren't the greatest.

Smiling Sheila

Loyal Rich,

It's been a while since I wrote.
I don't understand why you respond
sometimes and other times you
don't. My prayer is you're doing
well. My biggest concern is your
safety. I've already voiced my
concern about your drinking and I
won't be a nag.

It's important to me that I hear
from you and you keep in touch
with Rebecca. It was a big step
for you to write to her.
Something tells me you still love
her even after she hurt you.
We've been friends a long time.
So, I know if you didn't care for
her, you wouldn't bother.

I want you to understand
something. We all view people a
certain way based on our personal
experiences. Our flesh tells us
to judge another because they
didn't do what we want or they
don't live the way we think they
should live. We get so caught up
in ourselves that we don't see
another's point of view.

It takes effort to try to
understand where people's ideas
and opinions are coming from.

144

When someone hurts us, we get offended and immediately want to reject what they did or said. It's possible that our loved ones do certain things to protect us and we're not able to see it because we're too busy being offended.

Let me ask you this: Are you offended at what I just said? I want to invite you to put yourself in your sister's shoes that night when she called the ambulance. I wasn't there and can't tell you what was on her mind. According to her side, you were laid out on the couch, unable to move.

I say these things at the risk of losing your friendship. You're worth the risk. The reason is simple, you are one of God's trophies. He didn't give up on you and I firmly believe He put me in your life for that purpose too.

Please let me know how you're doing,

Concerned Kelly

Sheila,

I don't know how long I've been asleep, but it's nice to wake up to your soft voice and dainty fingers on my cheek. As I lift my head, I feel my head pounding. I should have taken something for it. I usually do so I can function the next day.

Looking through your windshield, I see it's still dark out. What time is it? If it's the middle of the night, I need to get home and get more sleep. I have 4 projects due in the next two weeks. I have to keep up or my boss will throw a fit.

I'm okay to drive home and I don't want to argue about it. Thank you for caring enough to keep me safe. I'll talk to you tomorrow or later today, depending on what time it is now.

Heading to my car,

Rich

Rich,

You're still drunk but at least your speech isn't slurred anymore. I wasn't going to allow you to drive when you couldn't even walk. I won't argue about you driving home, but I was hoping to see you after work. I love boating and kayaking. Can I talk you into ending work early tomorrow afternoon so we can have our first official date?

There it goes. I said it. I like you and I want to spend all the time I can with you. I don't expect you to be perfect, just someone I can be myself with. I don't know if you've been around the water back in Kansas City. Maybe it will be a new adventure.

I have so much time tomorrow, since I cut my visit with my family short. It was for the best. Having a nice day with you would be an added perk.

I hope to see you tomorrow,

Sheila

Sheila,

I've been sitting on the fence about allowing you to get close to me. We can talk more about that when I see you again. You're so beautiful I can't say no. If you want to take me on the lake, that's fine. I'm sure it will be interesting.

No, I've never been around the water. When you're tossed around from house to house, sleeping in strange beds, you don't get to do things like that. I'd love for you to show me the water.

I don't know about ending work early. I'm swamped all the time. If there is any way I can get away I will. Let's hope things slow down for me in the near future.

I'm not making excuses not to see you. I really want to see you outside of that noisy bar. I know…I choose to go there every night, but I need the outlet. Don't forget, if I didn't go in there, we wouldn't have met.

Let's set a time to meet in this parking lot, where you work. That way you can show me around. After all these years, I still don't know much about the area.

See you tomorrow,

Rich

Cute Rich,

It does my heart good that you chose me when you're so full of fear. Opening your heart to anyone isn't easy, especially considering what you've been through. You will have fun at Baker Lake. It's not far from here and the scenery is breathtaking!

I used to go to the open water, just north of Seattle. There's a little body of water called Puget Sound that leads to the Strait of Juan de Fuca. The border between the United States and Canada runs through the Strait. It's 95 miles long, so I could be out there all day without distraction.

I haven't gone there since I moved here. I had to search for another place to boat, and it's nice. You won't regret the experience.

I'm about to do the same thing as you, get some sleep. My bed is comfortable but lonely. It's gonna be a long night... what's left of it.

Anxious to see you,

Sheila

Sheila,

It's nice to see you after another stressful day. Sometimes I think I should have had my head examined when I chose this line of work. I got screamed at by a client for a simple error. I don't like to brag, but I'm one of the best in the business. It's not an ego trip, but I've been doing this for three lifetimes, it seems. There was no reason that guy should have thrown a fit like a 3-year-old, when I do such good work, as a rule.

Needless to say, I was glad to end my day early. I'll pick up where I left off either tonight or tomorrow morning. If that idiot wants to scream at me, he can wait with the rest of the money hounds.

Yes, I work for some big corporations. They request me specifically, which is why I never get a day off. The money is great, even better than when I started out here. A lot can change in a few years. It's the only thing keeping me going. I couldn't do this otherwise. Most people in my position have moved up to management, so they can boss around other people instead of doing the work themselves.

That's what I used to do in Kansas City. I was an executive manager. It was high stress too, but I didn't spend all day punching in data and creating new ideas for operating systems. I hired people to do that. Most of them get burned out after a few years, but keep doing it for the money.

Now that you've gotten me out on this boat, tell me about your job. You've heard me grumble enough about mine. It's giving me a headache. Now I need a drink.

Awaiting your response,

Rich

Grumbling Rich,

I don't know if I should laugh or smack you. If you're expecting me to feel sorry for you when you make all that money, you're crazy. I wish I could say I make great money. I'm not poor, but I sure wish I didn't have to live with a roommate. It's the only way I can afford the rent.

I'm sure you have your frustrations, but you own a house. It tells me you're doing well. That man who yelled at you was way out of line. There's no reason to talk to someone like that. We all have bad days, but it's over for you now.

My job is rough most of the time. When I started it a few years ago, I was fresh out of bartender school. I was nervous and wasn't used to interacting with a lot of people. It didn't take long to learn how many crazy people come to bars. I, too, didn't know if it was the right business for me, but here I am, still doing it.

Anyway, that's enough about work. Let's talk about you. You seem to be nervous. I'm hoping it's with the water and not being with me. I won't hurt you, I promise. Enjoy the snow caped mountains and the calm lake. It's the reason I come here.

I see you're not the aggressive type. I had to take your hand and invite you to touch me. It won't kill you to interlock fingers with me. You're so cute.

Now, if you don't mind, I'd like to talk about your family. What happened? How do they interact with you now?

I see your blank stare,

Concerned Sheila

Sheila,

You seem to be pretty canny, but a little harsh. Maybe I'm too sensitive, but if you've never walked in my shoes, you won't understand my struggles. I appreciate your concern, but I would rather talk about something else. I want to have a nice visit with you.

I love it here. I never paid attention to the mountains or anything else. I'm so caught up in work I don't have the time. Is there always snow on the mountaintops? It's funny how it's warm down here and I look up to see snow.

I'm glad we met. My family and friend in Kansas City all tell me I shouldn't go in the tavern and drinking is gonna kill me…blah-blah-blah. If I didn't go there, I would have never feasted my eyes on you.

I'm a little uneasy with this Lake experience. I've heard all these stories of shark attacks, I'd hate to be in tomorrow's paper. As long as you know what you're doing, I suppose I can trust you and relax.

How far do you go out? Do you head into the ocean? Oh, wait…you said we're on a lake…never mind. You can tell I don't get out much. I would love to travel the world someday, with the right person.

We've floated silently for about 5 minutes, just holding your soft hand. I've enjoyed soaking in the view and seeing the occasional critter running around. Who would've thought I would sacrifice an afternoon of work projects to do this?

Since you asked about my family, I'd like to ask about yours. You visit your dad every month, which is more than I care to do with my family. I don't even know my dad. I've never met him. I wish I didn't know the rest of them. I'm sure other people have more severe circumstances, but my family never wanted me around. That's why I moved here.

How about you? What's the beef with your brother and sister? Why would they treat you so poorly when you're such a sweet person?

Searching for answers,

Rich

Rich,

I'm glad you're enjoying being with me and learning to use the water for recreation. It's a shame you haven't done this before. Stick with me and I'll give you many more inspiring experiences. I think it's special that you chose to share it with me.

I don't mean to be harsh. I'm a blunt person. It comes from having to defend myself all my life. I understand the sibling rivalry thing, but I've got it bad, especially from my sister. She's so spiteful. Why do parents have to have more than one child? Don't laugh, you've thought it too, I'm sure.

I grew up in the busy city life. Everett is a sub-city of Seattle, so the traffic is heavy, and with it, comes stressed out people. That part I really don't miss. Although, I would put up with it before I would live near Sabrina and Sebastian again.

They always hated me because I was the go getter. In high school, I was deep into music and got to play in honors bands and orchestras in the county and state levels, even as a freshman. It's rare that a freshman gets to even audition. The awards started coming in and by the time I was a senior, I won the John Phillip Sousa and the Louis Armstrong awards. Both of them are very prestigious. Not many students get them...and I got both!

I was young and probably full of ego, but that was my dad's fault. He always encouraged me to be the best by getting me private lessons in piano and alto sax. Then I went to college to study music and did real well there for a couple years. I didn't finish. It's one of my biggest regrets.

I was so consumed by the way Sabrina and Sebastian treated me that I got into a relationship with this guy who was an athlete. He was in good shape and loved running cross country. His focus was on training for the Olympics, so I thought he was well put together. I was young and stupid.

Talk about being full of ego. All this guy ever talked about was how wonderful he was and all his ability. Then I caught him with another girl. He tried to lie to cover up, but I saw him with her. No need to go into detail, but I went from one bad relationship to another, until I finally gave up on men.

That's when I started going on the water: swimming, snorkeling, kayaking, canoeing, sailing. You name it, I did it. It was a good release and it made me forget my problems for a while. It felt good.

One day, I went out on the Strait of Juan de Fuca in a canoe to get some peace and quiet. I was really feeling down. The pain was like someone stabbed me with a knife. Then a boat approached me and a girl asked me if I was alright. She could see I was crying, but I didn't want to make a fool of myself in front of her whole crew. There were 5 or 6 of them.

She invited me to hang out with her and her friends for a while, so we docked and went to a tiki bar. We talked about my woes and she introduced me to the bartender who told me about how much fun I would have tending bar. I believed her, quit music school and went to bartender school.

I can't complain too much. It's fun most of the time...until the loud mouths and flirtatious guys come in. You'd be surprised what I hear from people when they've had too much to drink. Then again, you're in there every night, so you've heard them.

I'm not sure how all this sits with you, but I don't really know what I'm looking for in a man. You seem afraid to get involved and I am too. I guess the question is where we should take things from here.

This will be an interesting relationship,

Confused Sheila

Worrisome Sheila,

At this point, let's get to know each other. I don't care about your past. I've had it hard too. We all have a story we could live without.

It's good to hear you open up to me. It's not comfortable to reveal your dirty secrets to a stranger. Perhaps I won't be a stranger for long.

Tell me more about what there is to do on the water. How do you feel about going to the big waters again? I feel at home out here. It's too bad I didn't discover it sooner. The water in Kansas City looks kind of murky from what I see, but there are boats out there and I understand there's a lot of fish to catch.

The scenery here beats Kansas City by miles. The air is clean and the water is calm. On this clear day, I can see the mountains reflecting in the water. Even by the campsites it's quiet and not overcrowded. I've had quite a culture shock

160

since I moved to Washington State. I'll never go back to Kansas City.

I told you a little about my family problems that prompted me to move here. We can talk in depth anytime, I suppose. Since we have the rest of the day together, why not now. Get ready for a really unpleasant story.

Going deep,

Tired Rich

Hurting Rich,

Wow! I definitely see why you don't want your family around. I don't blame you for getting away from them. There was no reason for them to mistreat you. If they don't like your drinking, they should think for a while about the reason you drink. They drove you to it. You have to have something to relax and forget about the demons in your life.

You are a nice person who is obviously successful in business. They're miserable with themselves. People who are miserable can't stand to see other people happy. They hate to see anyone else get ahead in life. Forget about them and enjoy your new life.

We've just past the campgrounds where people like to hike. We could dock it and see the wildlife if you want. I'll leave it up to you. The trail runs 9 miles and goes up into the mountains. If you're in for some good exercise and exploration.

You don't look real enthusiastic about it, but you would forget about your problems for a while. I don't want to pressure you. Maybe what you have in mind is relaxing in the boat. No one understands that more than I do. That's why I took up boating, but I find hiking relaxing too.

I can never get tired of the sight of you. When I first saw you in the bar, I assumed you were another drunk that I didn't want to date, but it didn't stop me from checking you out. Then I got to know you a little. It didn't take long to realize you were timid and wanted to relax after work.

I'll ignore the two times you fell over. It bothered me, but I laugh about it now. You're just a silly guy with hot brown eyes.

Waiting for you to kiss me,

Sheila

Uplifting Sheila,

It does my heart good to hear you take my side about my family. I'm not used to that. Everyone else tells me I should sell my house and move back to Kansas City where I'm treated like a big nothing again. You, not only take the time to listen to me, but understand what I've been through.

I think your personal experience with your siblings helps you to empathize with me. I never knew how fortunate I was to meet you. I'll have to thank the old guy when I see him tonight. He encouraged me to pursue you. I was a nervous wreck and assumed you would either say no when I asked you out or you'd end up like all the other women I've come across. It helps to be broadminded, even at the risk of being hurt again.

I may be up to hiking sometime, but not today. I'm too tired and mentally drained. I hope you understand. I'd rather see where the river goes and take in the breathtaking mountain view.

I'll scoot a little closer to you, if you don't mind. I like your touch. It's been a long time since I've dated. I'm shaking as I hold you. Maybe it was a bad idea. I'm moving away again, to my side of the boat.

Embarrassed,

Rich

Vacillating Rich,

You are so cute. Don't be nervous with me. I'm nothing special. It's not like I'm the Queen of England or a movie star. Trying not to laugh at you takes some serious self-control.

If you're going to stay on the opposite side of the boat, I will have to come over there and get you. This is unfamiliar to me, being the one who pursues a guy. I'm used to all the guys chasing me. As strange as it is, I like coming after you.

You appear to have calmed down a bit. I think you're so afraid of rejection that you push people away. It's not going to work with me. Nice guys don't come around that often...at least not for me. Besides...all I want is to be held.

Aggressively,

Sheila

Beautiful Sheila,

Since you pressured me into it, I'll put my arms around you for a few minutes. If it makes me uncomfortable, I hope you will respect my wishes and back away. If you weren't so desirable, I wouldn't let you touch me at all.

I can't describe how it feels to scan the scenery while cuddling with you. I really thought I'd go the rest of my life without it. Being with a safe woman is foreign to me. I've had other relationships, but no one as sweet and caring as you. It's amazing what you learn from a person if you give them a chance.

People say we shouldn't build up walls to shut the world out. I get it, maybe a little more now, but I think it's wise to be cautious. I hate the thought of being taken advantage of again. I'll try not to think about it.

Enjoying your scent,

Rich

Sweet Rich,

I feel your pain and I don't want you to worry. The trauma my family put me through taught me a few things. When I got away from them, I promised myself I would never treat anyone the way they treated me. It wouldn't occur to my father to act like my brother and sister. They got that from our mother. She didn't say spiteful things to me, but I heard her talk to others that way more than once.

I don't want you to feel pressured to hold me. I can't make you like me, but I hope you will give me a chance. Who knows if we'll find love? Everyone wants it, so why fight it?

I get it, Rich. You're not the only one with fears. I took a break from dating too. There are too many nuts out there I needed to get away from. Thinking about the whole thing makes me tired.

Dating can be a full time job. I decided when I met another guy I was interested in, I would filter out all the addicts, control freaks, and religious nuts. All toxic people fall into one of those three categories...sometimes all three. It's taken many years of failed relationships, including with my own flesh and blood, to

168

realize the problem was me. I have to be able to choose good people.

I'm hoping the things I'm telling you is sinking in. We're not all that different, you and me.

Relaxing,

Sheila

Empathetic Sheila,

I would like to believe you are authentic and really want to know the real me. I'm not an easy person to read. Making an effort to enjoy life is a challenge. I love my house. It's quiet there. I can work hard and get my projects out without the drama of others. That's why my boss likes me and swamps me with work.

I know, I'm rambling about things we've already talked about. There's a reason for that. We've just met and already I feel a connection. The emotions get muddled. I have a bad habit of letting my family distract me from the joys of life.

I know you've told me not to let it bother me, but it's so hard. Even after I moved away, without telling any of them and making sure I'm never found, they manage to still bother me. The one person I did tell was a friend from back home who couldn't keep it quiet.

Now every week I get something in my mailbox from one or more of them, telling me how their "god" is the answer to all my problems, and then telling me everything I do is flawed. Who wants to follow a god who criticizes everything you do and insists you'll never measure up?

170

Every time I hear that hodgepodge I want to throw up. It makes me so mad. My poor excuse of a mother and sisters are so holier-than-thou, it gives them an excuse to tell me I'm the outcast.

Now that I'm in Washington State, they want me back home. It makes me sick. When I lived in Kansas City, I was a few miles from all of them and I was always pushed away. Now they insist I need the Lord. Where does all that come from? The only thing I need is to separate myself from them. I have a good life and it's going to stay that way.

I'm really not an angry person. It only comes out when I talk about those clowns. I'll calm down now before you start thinking I'm a raging bull. It's the opposite of how I feel when I'm with you…at least so far.

You smell nice…wait…I already said that,

Rich

Mixed up, Rich,

Yes, you mentioned that already. You're such a goofy man. I love it that you make me laugh. Thanks...I made a point to smell nice for you.

Now I see what's going on in your world. Your family isn't just mean-spirited, they're religious nuts. They all think they're better than anyone who doesn't believe exactly what they believe. I wish they would go to church and stay there. That way they can leave us alone.

We should all respect each other's opinions. I love who I am. I don't need a god to tell me what to do or who to love or what type of relationship to get into. I would respect Christians if they would respect me. Both of us know that day will never come.

I used to think you were quiet and I still do. I'm glad you chose to trust me with private information. It's good to be cautious, but don't allow it to push people away. There still are good people in the world.

We've reached the dock. The parking lot where we left our cars is on the other side of the boat rental. I hate to say goodbye, so why do we have to?

172

Let's have dinner at my place and we can talk some more.

What do you say?

Yearning Sheila

Sheila,

It's a tempting offer, but I'm going to say no. I want to spend more time with you, but let's choose a restaurant. We can still talk. This time we'll discuss more pleasant topics. I like to laugh and I'm sure you do too. Everyone likes to have fun.

If I go home now, I'll have to open my mailbox. It's always a stressful time. This way, I can put off the nagging letters.

Don't get me wrong, I don't want to use you as a way of escaping. I just want to take baby steps for now. The restaurants around here are never full in the middle of the week, only the bars. They fill up every night. It's funny how the moonlight heightens the alcohol cravings.

Since you tend bar for a living, let's go to that little Italian restaurant not far from here. The lights are low, giving it that romantic atmosphere. The Italians are experts in that department. I'm sure you've heard "That's Amore." There's a lot of truth in those lyrics. Italians love their food, wine, and women.

If that works for you, let's go,

Hungry Rich

174

Rich,

I'm okay if you're not ready for a relationship. If you think I asked you to my place with a hidden agenda, you're wrong. That's a little insulting. I've already told you how cautious I am with men because of all my bad breakups. If I said we could eat dinner and talk, that's all we will do.

Now, I see you shifting away from me. I'm not gonna bite you. Leaning against the car isn't going to repel me. You are so full of fear, but I'm telling you that's not a reason to distrust me. I'm not your mother or sisters. I'm Sheila...on your side.

I'm sure you've heard the saying, give love a chance. All I ask is for your trust...just a little bit. Women aren't all bad. I should know, I'm one of them.

Okay...I'm done chewing you out about it. If you want to go for Italian food, let's do it. I'm starved and it would be nice to continue our quiet time together. I'll drive.

Hungering for your time,

Sheila

FORGIVENESS IS A CHOICE

Insulted Sheila,

I was hoping you would understand. Initially, I thought you were gonna tell me to get lost. I don't think I can take another heartache right now. Thank you for keeping your mind open.

As we drive the short distance to the restaurant, I sense an awkward silence. Neither of us have spoken in the car. Hopefully, it's not because we don't have much to say to each other. It's too early in our relationship for that. We've arrived, so maybe the conversation, or the lack of it, will change.

The smell of the dining room reminds me of that little town I visited when I was on assignment in Perugia, Italy. The people there were friendly and went out of their way to welcome everyone to their table. They seem to take pride in hospitality.

It's the same feel here. They know me by face and take care of me. These Italians love to talk, but they quickly learned, I'm not much for conversation. The food is excellent and it's quiet. You won't find a bar scene in this place.

It's nice sitting here with you. Seeing your pretty face across the table makes me forget my past. If only it would stay that way. The dim candlelight compliments your beautiful eyes and full lips. I don't know why you're wasting your time with me. My baggage is packed to the ceiling and I'm afraid it will fall on you.

I want to trust you and I'm sure all women aren't bad. There are approximately 7 billion people in the world. There's no way I could get to know all of them.

We agreed to talk about something pleasant during dinner, so let's start now. Forget about our past and our struggles. Tell me about your future. What do you see yourself doing? I will try to open myself up a little more after a couple of glasses of wine.

Enjoying your company,

Rich

Pleasant Rich,

I'm glad you finally decided to relax. That seems to be a big struggle for you. This is a nice restaurant. The atmosphere is perfect...and you don't look too bad yourself. To be honest, when I first noticed you in the tavern, I was hoping you would pursue me. You're really cute.

It's nice to see a smile. I was wondering if you were capable. Life goes by so fast, why waste it being miserable?

With that said, this nice restaurant reminds me of the last time I ate in one. We already talked about that. I really don't want to discuss my siblings anymore. Getting to know you is much more pleasant. Heck...just looking at you makes me forget the ugliness in my life.

I'm not worried about your baggage, as you call it. We all have a story. Sometimes I think people are born mean. There's nothing you can do about it but stay away from them. Now, I'm not going to say another word about that.

How about you hold my hand while we wait for our food? I don't care what anyone says, there's not enough touching in the world. If everyone was open about touching, they wouldn't have so much stress in their lives.

I need your affection,

Sheila

Sultry-Eyed Sheila,

Your fingers are thin and soft. It's making it difficult to relax. I haven't touched a woman in a long time. I know it's only your hand, but… I guess it's okay.

Now that the food is here, you'll have to let go so we can eat. I need two hands. Dinnertime discussions tend to be boring. That's why I eat alone most of the time. Actually, I find it easier to do most everything without menacing people around. You already know that.

Maybe it's fate that brought me here to Washington. I was running from my problems, but what if it's part of a master plan. Do you believe in such things? I have a friend, Kelly, back in Kansas City who is a Christian. All I hear about is Jesus and god in Kelly's letters.

I'm sure I will go home to a full mailbox. Everyone keeps trying to convince me to move back home. They don't realize, this is my home. I'm a grown man with an excellent career, a nice house that's paid for, and now, a beautiful woman in my life. It's nice to know I found a place where I fit in.

I see you sitting there with deep thoughts. Tell me what's on your mind. I know I talk too much sometimes, so I'll shut up now.

Anticipating your response,

Rich

Silly Rich,

You make me laugh. You don't have to shut up. I like hearing what you have to say. That's the only way I can get to know you.

It impresses me how confident you are about your career. It's interesting how you've been to different places around the world...and you get paid for it. The closest I've come to traveling was an application I put in for a cruise job. They didn't hire me.

Underneath that confidence is an average guy afraid to be himself. I understand how that feels. Being criticized all my life made me want to flee and your being forced into foster care has the same effect. We have a lot of hurt feelings coming into this relationship, but I like to think we're two puzzle pieces that fit together. We're both unique individuals that happen to meet by coincidence.

That brings me to your question about god. I mentioned it before, but I try not to think about it. I don't really care for Christians. They love Jesus and hate everyone else. Religion causes all the problems in the world. Hitler was a Christian. He was baptized as a baby, went

182

through the sacraments, and the list goes on. A lot of good that did him, not to mention, the millions of innocent people he killed.

If you're asking my opinion about Christianity, I think it's a crock of crap. Everyone needs to feel comfortable with the people they hang around. I understand that...but I shake my head at those church going idiots. How can anyone be so naive?

If there's a god, he needs to show his face. Don't they say god made us in his image? If that were true, someone must have verified it thousands of years ago. Where is he now? Show me the proof. All I see is a world full of drunk idiots I have to serve and play nice to every night, just to pay the rent.

If there's a god who is so powerful, this world wouldn't be such a sorry place. Wars are caused all throughout history. What's the purpose? War accomplishes nothing. Where's god when all that is happening? You've got to be a pretty blind person to believe in an almighty god (I say while rolling my eyes) who lets so much hardship go on in the world.

I could go on, but now I'm the one rambling. It's a waste of my breath to talk about it. The churches aren't going anywhere. In fact, every minute a new church is being built, it seems.

You've gotten to see a side of me that I try to hide. I'm not always angry, believe it or not. It's only certain things that get under my skin. You'll learn I just stay away from problem people, and Christians are the most problematic people in the world. That's why the Middle East hates us.

Let's not discuss that anymore. I'm sorry you had to see all that anger. I didn't mean to bite your head off about it. You're so sweet to listen. It's nice to have someone who will let me get things out. Have you ever felt like screaming because no one cares how you feel?

Trying to enjoy my meal,

Sheila

Wild Sheila,

Well…I definitely see you've had all that bottled up for a long time. It's a relief you feel the same way I do. You don't need to apologize. I understand where you're coming from. It sounds like you and I will have a great relationship. I never thought it would happen.

You made a mess of your lasagna. How many forks do you have? It looks like the Coast Guard came and massacred it. It's ok…that's the good thing about most Italian dishes, they taste the same no matter how you mix it…or in your case, destroyed it.

I'm glad we agree on most things…at least, so far. I want to disagree on one thing you said. I'm not afraid to be myself. The world doesn't let me be myself. It's not worth the fight to claim freedom. I just end up frustrated and ready to kick someone into oblivion.

Now that we've finished eating, I'll pay the bill. I hate this day to end. It's been wonderful. I've never been so at peace. Don't look so surprised, it's the truth. How about we take a nice walk while there's still an hour or so of daylight left? I would ask to take you for a drink, but you've got to be sick of that environment. One day it will end.

Prolonging the day,

Rich

LETTERS FROM SECLUSION

Patient Rich,

You are so funny. Anyone else would run as far as they could if they saw me take my anger out on a delicious piece of lasagna. Thanks for sticking around. I think a walk would help me calm down. Let's drive to the docks again and walk by the water. It's peaceful there...as we've already discussed.

Again, the car ride was quiet. Oh well...

You're such a gentleman to open my door for me. I hope you're not just trying to impress me. Everyone is excited when they get into a new relationship. It seems you want this as much as I do. I wasn't so sure at first. This has been a nice day.

Thanks for holding my hand as we walk along the bank. I have to say, I've never done this with anyone.

You asked what I want to do in the future. I don't know. I think about going to school to become a hairdresser. It's expensive and I wouldn't make that much more. I'm making $22,000 a year with my tips. Some stylists make close to $30,000, but that's rare, from what I understand.

I'm at a loss as to what to do with my future. Maybe I'll meet a rich man so I can be the housewife and stay-at-home mom. That's every woman's dream. I'm probably gonna be stuck with tending bar the rest of my life. I'm okay with that, I guess. I'm grateful for my career. At least, I have one. There are so many people out there who have no skills and work for minimum wage their whole life.

Complacent,

Sheila

Sheila,

I don't know what to say about your future goals. Sometimes we must accept life as it comes. Do me a favor and don't give up on the dream. There's always a chance it will happen anyway…without a rich man.

The sun is almost down, so we better head back to the cars. It's even darker trying to find our way through the trees. I'll hold on to you so we don't get separated. Take your time.

We can use the light over the horizon to guide us in the right direction. The parking lot can't be far.

You must be afraid. Your grip is tighter than it was a few minutes ago. Please don't panic, we'll find it soon. I can still hear the water on our right side, so we're not lost.

I see the clearing, which means the cars are parked close by. Even I can relax. Yes, I admit, I was a little concerned about finding our way back. We shouldn't have walked so far when we knew the sun would set soon. I guess we were having fun.

I notice you still have your firm grip around my waist. Are you afraid?

What's up?

Rich

Strong Rich,

I knew you were as scared as I am. I will hold you until we get back to my car. That way I know I'll get home safely. I guess every woman needs something to hold. I chose a nice looking, brave man, and I'm not letting go.

You can't see my smile in the dark, but it's there. Now that you helped me find my car, I want you to kiss me. Is that too much to ask?

I feel you are timid or shy with me. I can feel your body shake. What are you afraid of? I may be a lot of things, but a cannibal isn't one of them. For someone who brags about his career, I don't get why you're afraid of a little intimacy. Whatever the case, I can handle it. Like I said, I'm not letting go of you.

Can I ask you one more time to come to my place for a couple drinks? I know you said no, and I don't want to pressure you, but I will be alone tonight, without my obnoxious roommate. It would be nice to end the evening relaxing with you.

I'll let you decide,

Sheila

LETTERS FROM SECLUSION

Rebecca,

I guess you must care about me since you won't go away. Even when I ignore you, the letters never stop. It's like a gnat that keeps flying in your face, no matter how many times you swat at it.

I had an amazing time yesterday with a beautiful woman. It was such a perfect day, I didn't want to spoil it by opening my mailbox. I knew it would be full of annoying letters from my family.

I read back through the last couple of letters you wrote. You keep bringing up the night when I went to the hospital. Do you think I need you to remind me? I'll admit I was more embarrassed than hurt. I never wanted you to find me passed out and I understand you were scared. If you didn't come by, I may have died. I get it.

Yes…I think about all the nights we stargazed. You were the only person who took the time for me. We laughed a lot, but it was always interrupted by the foster home situation. When it was time to leave, all the laughter and joy was gone. It was like a huge eraser came and wiped it all away.

I never fit in anywhere. All these years and I finally found my home. Washington is so much fun. I love this small town and some of the people I've met here.

Last night, I had a long talk with a special lady, Sheila. She's the bartender at the bar I go to every night after work. I know what you're thinking. *She's not the right woman for you...blah, blah, blah.* You're wrong, this time. Sheila pushed me to write you.

She has her struggles with her family too, which is why we get along. I don't know why, but I must have said something that prompted her to encourage me to keep in touch.

So, I've done it. You and Sheila got me to write. I don't know whether to say, I hope you write or just leave me alone. I know the latter will do me no good.

Until your next letter,

Rich

Rich,

I heard from your sister, Rebecca. She was thrilled that you didn't attack her, as you have in the past. I'm sure you will hear back from her, if you haven't already. It's hard to tell what you're thinking, but I'm glad you've made an effort to mend your relationship.

I just got back from a great weekend. My parents treated their kids and grandkids to one of the best weekends I've had in a long time. We stayed at an expensive water resort. It had everything...not only lots of water slides, but video games and three restaurants. All of it was inside the hotel building!

It wasn't only fun for my niece and two nephews. The adults all got in on the indoor waterpark. This is what family time is all about. My parents wouldn't let anyone pay for a thing. I offered to pay for dinner Saturday night, but dad made it clear he was buying.

I'm still on a high from the experience. I've never laughed so

FORGIVENESS IS A CHOICE

much in one weekend. God sure is good to me. He has blessed me so much through the years, even with all my shortcomings. The Lord brought me out of a pit of disaster, with the drug problem, and turned me into one of His trophy pieces.

There was one thing that would have made it a perfect experience. As much fun as I had, I really wished you were there. My mom and dad have each other and my brother has his family. I was there alone. Having a friend there may not be the same as having a spouse, but it's better than being alone.

Thinking of the days when we used to hang out, just because we liked each other's company, takes me to a place of multiple emotions. One part of me wants to rejoice (I do smile and even chuckle every now and then), but it always ends in sadness.

I miss those times. It was quite a few years ago, but I still remember every minute. We had our share of arguments, but we always remained friends. God puts people in our lives for His purposes and I'm convinced He put you in my life.

Ups and downs are part of a relationship. Don't let what happened with your mother destroy the wonderful relationships you made here in Kansas City. There are lots of people who adore and need you.

I know you don't like to hear about God, but He is the center of my life. Maybe you're thinking I will eventually give up trying to convince you Jesus is real. My answer to that is, He never gave up on me so I'll never give up on you.

I will continue to pray for you and your family. Most of all, I will be on my knees, reminding myself God is in control.

Please write back soon,

Kelly

Mentor,

It's about time you got here. You usually beat me in and have a table warmed up for us. I'm on my third margarita already. A lot has happened in the last 24 hours. The day with Sheila was awesome. She's a sweet person.

It amazes me how much we have in common. Her family is looney. She told me all about them. What is it about family taking you for a ride?

You're laughing at me. I figured you would. I'm glad I can constantly amuse you. That won't spoil my good mood. You encouraged me to go after her, so laugh at yourself.

Have a beer. I'm buying tonight. I had another long day at work. It's time to unwind.

I see Sheila isn't here yet. She'll be along in a few minutes. It's not the same with this old man that works in the afternoon. I think he's the owner or a friend of the owner.

Heading to the bar,

Rich

Young Fella,

I'm not laughing at you to be cruel.
Sometimes you can be so defensive. I
think it's good that you're happy.
Heck...one of us might as well enjoy our
life. As you come back to our table with
my beer and, yet another margarita for
you, I think of myself at your age. I
thought life was full of excitement every
time I met some girl.

Now I'm a broken down old drunk. What
did it do me? Women used to like me,
now it's a thing of the past. I'll die
alone...just me and my beer.

Forget I said all that. I'm just jealous.
Tell me what you two did before she gets
in here. No doubt, she will be peering at
you all night, watching everything you do
and say.

Sorry to be a downer,

Mentor

Jealous Mentor,

At least you have the guts to admit it. Most men are too full of pride to say they're jealous. I'm sorry for your bad luck, but it won't stop this night from being the best one we've had together in a while. Enjoy a night of free beer and conversation.

Sheila and I went boating on Baker Lake. It was interesting since I've never been in a boat before. An added plus was being in close proximity to a beautiful woman. We talked and she showed me the nice views. It was really relaxing, which is something I don't do much.

Then I got to see a side of her at dinner which blindsided me. She got mad while discussing her family and…well let's say, I'm glad I wasn't on her plate. She can get violent with a fork.

Then she wanted me to come to her place. She kept hinting about it all day. I wasn't comfortable, but I finally said yes. Then we talked at nauseam about my family and Kelly. It bothered me at first, but I tried to hide it. I didn't want to argue with her on our…wait! She's here!

Acting natural,

Rich

Nervous Rich,

I have to shake my head. Will you relax? She's not a celebrity. Well, maybe she is in this bar. All the guys check her out and hit on her after a few drinks. I can see by your hard look you want me to shut up about it. Fine...I'll play it cool.

There she goes...walking by you with a nice smile. I'll bet she couldn't wait to get to work tonight. Look at you...you're blushing. You remind me of those old cartoons where the boy bird's heart is pounding through his chest for the girl bird.

I shouldn't rag you. It's just fun. Like I told you, it will fade.

Enjoy the moment,

Mentor

Annoying Mentor,

You really are jealous. Who are you to say whether this relationship will fade? She could be the one I'm supposed to be with the rest of my life. I know everything we've talked about. It hasn't escaped me. What if you're wrong about people? Can they all really be bad?

You know, that talk Sheila and I had about my family? Well, she told me to keep in touch with my sister. It never dawned on me, and I don't know why, but she cares enough to write me, even though I dismiss her. I think there's some love there. It may be in a really warped way, but there must be a reason she wants to keep a relationship with me.

I appreciate all the advice you've given me. Really…I do. I'm just thinking there has to be good people in this world. The planet earth is a huge place. I should know, I've traveled it enough.

The people I ran into in Italy were great. The Italians think nothing of welcoming you into their homes and feeding you. They'll tell you their whole life story in the first 10 minutes. You laugh, but it's true.

I could go on about all the exotic places I've visited, but I won't. My work has taken me around the world. That job I had in Kansas City was high pressure, but I made good money. Of course, I make about the same here, only because I work long hours. It wasn't that way when I started, but work has picked up considerably. I think I've mentioned this before.

I guess, what I'm saying is…I don't know what I'm saying. I think I'm questioning where I am in my life and where I'm going. I mean…what's the point in living if all we do is work and get drunk…and all along, hate people in general?

I still want to hear your thoughts on all this,

Inquisitive Rich

Naïve Rich,

Listen to yourself. You have one date with a pretty girl and she has you railroading into believing a bunch of garbage. So, you had a good time. I'm glad you did...but don't let Sheila change your views.

Your mother, the only woman who gave birth to you, tossed you out with the trash. She might as well of had an abortion. It's the same thing. Are you worth throwing away?

You can believe me when I say, there are no good people in the world. They will take advantage of you and then toss you in a blender. No one does things for you unless there's something they can get out of it. Do you go to work for free? No! You do it for the paycheck.

What is it about you young, naive boys? You see a pretty face and go all gaga. You're pathetically predictable. I know because I used to be one of them. I'm not so old that I can't remember what it felt like to hold a woman or kiss a woman.

I'm not trying to hurt your feelings, kiddo, but that bartender is after one thing. It's the same thing they all want...money. Let me lean in so you can hear me in this noisy tavern. If you think she's different than other women, just wait until she starts grabbing at your 401K and whatever else.

Trust me, I know. I was left with nothing, thanks to my ex-wife. I gave her 42 years of supporting her and our 2 boys, only to end up in divorce court. What for? Over alcohol. She couldn't control my desire to drink a couple beers after work, so she abandoned me.

I think it was all in her plan. That criminal...and I call her that because she robbed me of thousands of dollars...took half our house, that she never paid a dime for, got all of my IRA, and made sure both our kids hated me when it was all over. That's the thanks you will get for serving and loving a woman.

Not that you got me upset, I think I'll sit at the bar for a while,

Infuriated Mentor

Upset Mentor,

Hey! Wait a minute. You don't have to run off. Come sit back down. I won't bring it up again. I had no idea all that happened to you.

I'll give you a bit to calm down, then I want to ask you a question.

Okay…we've watched TV without speaking for about a half hour. Let me ask you something. Back in the beginning, when you saw I was interested in Sheila, you encouraged me to pursue her. Now you're telling me she's gonna "rob" me, to use your words. That doesn't make much sense.

If you're worried about me, I can understand it, but there's more to this than you looking out for me. It's obvious you're still bitter about your divorce. I'm sorry that happened to you…really.

You haven't said a word to me. It's not like you. I suppose I'll call it a night then, after I finish my drink.

Patting you on the shoulder,

Rich

My dear brother, Rich,

Tell me more about Sheila. It seems she is special to you. No, I'm not going to automatically say she's not right for you, just because she works in a bar. I will say, a sister needs to know how she treats you and how she views life.

If you feel that your life in Washington is where you need to be, I will do my best to accept it. It would be nice to see you again or talk to you on the phone. It's up to you. Don't hear me trying to pressure you.

Life here is the same. I still love my home. It's quiet and I still sit on the porch after everyone is in bed. It's my only "me time." I find myself spending a great deal of it thinking about what to write you next or wondering if you will ever write me again.

LETTERS FROM SECLUSION

I'm praising God right now. He opened your heart enough to talk to your favorite sister.

Encouraged,

Rebecca

Rebecca,

I see you've been talking to Kelly. It's okay with me. She's been a good friend…and I do miss the time I used to spend with the both of you. I admit, I've been stubborn and a bitter person.

Apparently, you don't understand. I was treated like the outsider… I was the only one of mom's kids who was abandoned. I'm forced to live with the fact that my own mother, who carried me for 9 months, didn't think enough of me to want to raise me. She raised the rest of her kids. What's wrong with me that I was a reject as soon as I took my first breath?

Now, I'm getting upset all over again. That's why I don't talk about it. This sucks.

You asked about Sheila. I don't know what to say. We just started dating, but I've known her for a long time. Like I said, she tends bar at the tavern where I hang out every night. We laugh together a lot and have similar views.

I know you believe in God, but Sheila and I are on the same page. It's hard to believe in a God who would let so much crime, hatred, etc. happen in this world. Isn't he supposed to be all powerful?

Right now, I think it's a big step for me to date. I thought I would never get close to anyone again.

You are right about one thing…she is special. Even though she's a bartender, she's smart and passionate. I smile just thinking about her.

I'm sure you're shaking your head right now, but I will continue to see Sheila. Don't worry, I'm fine and she won't lead me down the dark road of destruction.

I know how you think,

Smiling Rich

Little Brother, Rich,

I've always tried to keep an open mind with your girlfriends, as I do with everything I do. Everyone is entitled to their opinion. I won't say much about Sheila. I've never met her.

I wish I knew more about the town where you live. I can't even picture what it's like to spend all your time with little traffic and not much to do. Big city is all I know. At least you're near the water.

I have to take care of my family now, Rich. I wish I could write more. I'd like to tell you all about my husband and your niece and nephew.

Please be careful,

Rebecca

LETTERS FROM SECLUSION

Kelly,

I haven't been ignoring you. I spent the last two weeks thinking. I wrote back to Rebecca. It seems, she doesn't know what to say to me. The only thing I get from her is a bunch of questions. I know why, too. She wants to get enough information out of me to figure out where I'm living. I didn't tell her anything.

I have to say, it was nice to talk to her. I told her I wasn't mad at her anymore for calling 911. I guess you could say, she's the second person who saved my life. You two had to have something in common.

She's keeping her mouth shut about my dating a bartender. There's no doubt she wants to ream me out. I appreciate her staying out of it. Believe me, this is the first time in her life she didn't meddle in my business.

I'm glad you had a good time with your family. I'm flabbergasted your dad wanted to shovel out some dough over the weekend. He must have gotten a big bonus at work, or something. You deserve to be spoiled every now and then.

It did my heart good to hear that you missed me. I know you never married and see your other siblings with families of their own. It's bound to

211

brew some jealousy. Look at me, I never married either. You're not so old that you'll die an old maid. There's no point in both of us leading a life of despair.

Don't you have your faith to lean on? You spend so much time talking about it, I thought that was enough. What are you supposed to do when life isn't fair?

I've been pondering this idea of faith lately. I keep thinking about my life. I work long hours, 7 days a week, and sit in that little tavern every night, getting drunk. Yes, I admit, I get drunk…a lot. What kind of life is that?

Even Sheila, the bartender I'm dating, has goals. I make such good money that I have no need for goals. My house is paid for, I have tons of cash in the bank, and a good-looking retirement account. Many people would say I have everything. Do I? I started dating, so I must want something more out of life than taking care of myself.

If there is a God, where is He when I'm confused? Why didn't He come down and comfort me when I screamed into the sky because I thought I was all alone, with no one who cared about me? My only resource was to start a new life in a new town. Why didn't He stop my mother from kicking me to the curb?

Enough of the questions. No one can answer them. Many have tried to no avail. I'm just wondering why I was put on this earth. If no one wants me around, except drunks and one woman who makes the drunkenness possible, what's the point?

Now that I've officially depressed you, I'll say goodbye for now. This is the main reason I don't like to talk about faith and the value of my life. I think I will have to take more time to figure it out.

Don't be offended if I don't write for a while,

Angry Rich

Rich,

It saddens me to see you so disgusted with the world. I can't explain all the bad things that happen. I wish I could. Sometimes I shake my head and wonder what God is doing, but I know He is still on the throne. He is still in control.

I shed some tears after reading your letter. It probably doesn't make any difference to you. That's okay.

Anyway…the struggles you have aren't uncommon. I know it feels like running away was your only option, but, as I'm sure you noticed, your problems followed you there.

I don't say these things to upset you. Believe me…I'm upset enough for the both of us. You didn't deserve to be rejected by so many foster families…and your mom. There's one thing you're overlooking. You're spending so much time thinking about what went wrong that you can't see the blessings God has given you.

I know it's not what you want to hear, but it's the truth. You have a sister and a good friend, in me, who want you in our lives. And, believe it or not, your mother does too. The mistakes she made were severe and she can't go back and erase them. I don't expect you to easily forgive your mother. I get it.

I don't know what it will take to make you understand that you're loved. I know life can be a dark place, but it doesn't have to stay that way. It's a choice you have to make.

If you decide not to write for a while, I will respect your wishes. The prayers are coming your way in the meantime.

Jesus loves you more than you know,

Patient Kelly

FORGIVENESS IS A CHOICE

Sheila,

We've been seeing each other for several months now. I don't know how you feel about me, but I still think you're a wonderful woman. You've fulfilled the void I've been missing. After a horrible childhood and not much better adulthood, until now, I can finally say I have a great life.

You've opened my heart to so many new adventures, not only on the water, but learning how to laugh. That's a new concept to me. I've never had anything to be joyful about.

My workload has slacked off, a bit, which is a good thing. I can spend the extra time with you.

I know you don't like to talk about your job, for good reason. There will be a day when you don't have to tend bar anymore. I don't mean to laugh about it, but being negative isn't in my vocabulary anymore.

I can't wait to see you again,

Content Rich

Rich,

Wow! I'm confused and flattered. I thought we were just hanging out. You didn't seem all that interested in me. Now you're telling me about your strong feelings for me. It makes me smile, but I don't understand you at all.

I'm sorry...you never touch me unless I touch you first. Even then, you don't really respond. In the 6 months I've dated you, we've spent 2 dates at my place and I've never seen yours.

That's really confusing, Rich. You live alone. I have a roommate. It would be easier to go to your house to eliminate distractions. It's like you're afraid I'm after your money or something. If I could get you alone, I would show you how much I love you.

I'm happy to hear your true feelings for me. I was wondering what was going on in your head.

I have to ask you: Why are you so afraid of a woman's touch. You should know by now that I don't want anything but your love...including your intimacy. Rich, you tell me all the time how beautiful I am. I would think you would want me physically. You're a man! I thought that's all you guys think about, day and night.

Do you love me?

Sheila

Sheila,

When we meet tonight, I will discuss this with you. I'm sorry I have a problem with expressing myself. I've been in a shell for so long, it's hard to crack open the egg.

I just finished my work week. The work is slacking off even more. There's no work on Saturday and Sunday anymore. I was just informed. I hope I'll be okay. Not that money is a worry. I just don't plan on retiring for another 20 years. What would I do with myself when I'm used to working long hours?

Obviously, I'm worried. The good thing is I was smart enough to save 85% of my earnings over the 5 and a half years I've been here. Plus, I had money left over from the sale of my Kansas City house.

I know you don't like my bragging about my financial situation, but I'm really not bragging. I'm still a relatively young man. What if my income stops? Will there be a future for us?

Yes, I love you,

Rich

PART 2

Family Ties

Rich,

I know you wanted some time to ponder your faith and living situation, but you really need to hear this. Mom is in the hospital. She had a massive stroke. There's a slim chance she will survive. If she does survive, she won't be able to take care of herself.

By the time you read this, it may be too late to see mom alive. It's up to you, but your family really needs you. Don't shut us all out. It looks bad.

You can stay at my house while you're here. We would love to have you. The kids and my husband would love to meet you.

Please consider coming on the first available flight,

Rebecca

LETTERS FROM SECLUSION

Sheila,

I'm sorry to cancel our date, but I have an emergency. My mother is in critical condition. From what my sister, Rebecca, tells me, our mom won't make it.

I will make it up to you when I return. Please pray for my mother and my family.

I love you,

Rich

Rebecca,

I've decided to come to Kansas City. This is awkward after all these years, but I have to see mom before she passes away. There's plenty I would like her to know. There's even more I want to ask her.

I'm leaving tomorrow afternoon and will arrive at MCI airport around 10pm. It was the earliest Kansas City flight I could find. I hope everyone will hold up okay until then…including mom.

I will keep her in my prayers. As much as I question the reality of God, it's something I will have to ponder at another time. If there is a God, I hope He hears our prayers.

I'll rent a car from the airport, so you don't have to cart me around. I should be at your house around 11pm.

Take care until then,

Rich

Bailing Rich,

I'm sorry about your mother. I know it's been a long time since you've seen her. It will be really weird, but if you feel like you have to see her before she dies, go.

I don't want to add any stress to your plate, but I'd like to go with you. Apparently, I need to tell you this, instead of thinking of it on your own. I want to be there to support you through this.

Considering everything that's happened, it will be a hard time for you. Don't you think? I don't want to sound angry, but it hurts my feelings that you want to push me away at such a tough time.

I understand about breaking our date. I hope everything ends up okay. I'll look forward to seeing you when you get back.

Please be safe,

Sheila

FORGIVENESS IS A CHOICE

Sheila,

You're right about one thing, it is a trying time. I'm shaking my head right now. The reason is clear to most people. I can't believe you would jump me about not thinking of you. That's enormously selfish. I know you've had problems with men, but that doesn't mean you get to attack me during a time of crisis.

For you to say, "I don't want to add any stress to your plate," is an understatement. I can't believe some of the things you come up with sometimes. I love you dearly, but I may need to rethink who you are right now.

The reason I didn't ask you to come was because of my family. I don't know how they will take to you, especially my sister Rebecca. She has a knack for ruining my relationships. No woman is ever good enough for me, in her eyes, so she tries to wedge me away from whoever I'm dating.

I didn't want you caught in the middle of her toxicity. That's just one of the issues I have with my family. Rebecca is the least of the problems. My other 3 sisters never wanted me around. They always made a game out of picking on me.

Becoming an adult didn't stop any of that. When I told everyone I was going to college to study

226

computer programing, they all laughed in my face. It was their way of telling me I would never be anything but a loser.

Now I make more money than all of them put together. Not that it matters. They still think I'm an outcast. It's the reason I started drinking. I'm glad I left, but now I feel like home is where I belong. I can't escape those clowns, no matter what I do.

So, you see. This is why I don't want you to come with me. You don't deserve to be treated like that. Yes…they will snarl at you the same as me, just because we're dating. You don't deserve that.

Don't ever doubt how I feel about you. Okay?

Stressed out Rich

Rich,

You're making me cry. I know you only told me how you feel, but it was harsh. I didn't mean to sound selfish. You are so special to me I want to be there with you, so you don't have to handle it all alone.

It's sweet of you to consider my needs first. I had no idea you were so thoughtful. I'm really a big girl and can handle myself. If you don't want me to come, I won't take it personally. Besides, I don't know if my heartless boss would let me off, even during such a bad time.

I want to see you before you leave. It will do me good to hold you. I can take you to the airport before work.

I'm sorry for upsetting you,

Sheila

LETTERS FROM SECLUSION

Rebecca,

You look different after all these years. Your home looks the same as I remembered, except for the furniture. It looks lived in. It amazes me how much stuff people accumulate through the years. When the kids come, it's even worse.

I don't know if I should hug you. Would you be okay with that?

Kansas City looks the same. The traffic is still a mess. I don't miss that. Every big city has that problem. I've been to enough of them to know.

I've had a long day, so if it's all right with you, I want to get some sleep,

Rich

Rich,

Opening the front door and seeing you standing there made my heart sing. Sorry for getting teary eyed. I instantly realized how much I missed you. A big part of me was empty...I uh...I don't know what else to say. It's so good to see you.

I know it's late, but I would really like to talk while my family is asleep. Even though we've been writing, I feel there is so much to say. Letters can't convey the fulfillment of having your little brother close to you.

I'm glad you're safe and doing well. I'm proud of your success in business. It's hard to believe that little boy I grew up with would turn into a millionaire. Most people would kill to achieve so much.

My husband is a little nervous to meet you. He's heard different things about you, so doesn't know how he will react to seeing you for the first time. He's a little shy, but that's what I love about him.

I keep shifting in my seat. I guess I'm a little nervous to have you here too. You haven't said 2 words since you greeted me at the door.

What's going on in your head?

Rebecca

Big Sis Rebecca,

I'm not much for words, as you know. I too feel awkward being in your house. The last time I was here, you were alone, and now you have a family. If only I was that lucky.

We can talk more tomorrow. I want to rest now. Let me ponder things, just as I did on the flight here.

Now that I'm settled in bed, I'll do what I do best…write. I suppose it was a good thing you and I kept in touch through the mail. It wouldn't have happened if you didn't make the effort. I'm grateful.

I was hurt for a lot of years, feeling like you betrayed me. I don't have to go into detail about that night in the hospital. We've discussed it too many times. I understand by calling the ambulance, you saved my life.

I can't remember every detail…actually very little about that night, and it doesn't matter. I'm trying hard to put the past behind me. I hope you can too.

We need to concentrate on mom right now, hence the reason I came. I don't know how she will react to seeing me. It probably won't be pleasant. Although, what can she say after having a stroke?

I'm shaking my head trying to absorb everything. All this is overwhelming. I will keep up my guard when I see everyone. This family is as dysfunctional as they come.

I'll try to get some sleep now. It's only a few hours until dawn. I hope I can rest.

Until the a.m.,

Rich

Mom,

I've seen this hospital many times. My last visit prompted me to move away. Walking into the lobby, I see the information desk. Mrs. Portilla is still working there. She always made me laugh when I was a kid. Is she ever going to retire?

Why do hospitals always smell the same? This place brings back some memories; some good, some not so good. I'm not sure I want to go up to your room. It's down the same hall I was on when I broke my arm, thanks to my spiteful oldest sister.

You can thank Rebecca for getting me here. If she didn't persist by writing me, even though I didn't want it, I wouldn't have seen how much she wanted to reconnect.

All is quiet on the way to your room. Rebecca keeps looking at me, as to say, you're going to see your mother, whether you like it or not. I'm not arguing. I made it this far. It would be silly not to visit you after coming all this way.

I paused as I saw the opened door to your room. Rebecca grabbed my arm, insisting I go in. Who am I to argue with my big sister?

I got a chill as I entered. I can't help but think of the last time I saw you. We had a big blow up and the next thing I did was move away without saying goodbye. I guess all that doesn't matter now.

As the tension builds, so does the stench,

Rich

Rebecca,

I'm sorry I left mom's room abruptly. I felt like an ostrich with its head in the sand. It was too awkward to see her laying there, unresponsive. I don't know if she ignored me or really couldn't say anything.

It felt like another bitter, backstabbing act on her part. How do I know she wasn't snubbing me for disappearing? I guess I will have to wait until she wakes…if she wakes.

If she dies, my trip out here will be for nothing. I'm sorry, but I couldn't stay in there and watch the IV drip, listen to the beeps from the machines, or watch mom stay in the same position without moving even a little. She might as well be dead if that's all her life will entail.

I keep calling her mom. As I write this, it irks me to no end. There were so many mothers in my life, I lost count. What does that mean? I don't know. What do I know? As I rub my forehead, I'm thinking about all the mothers who had me for a little while, and then booted me back to the shelter.

Please don't get mad at me. All the hurt feelings are coming back. It's more than I can take. Life in Washington is good…no, it's great. I should have never come back here.

I'll be back to your place later,

Rich

Appalling Rich,

That's exactly what your behavior was today, Appalling...no horrendous! Here I was so proud of you for making this big step to come see mom and your family again. I don't know what to say. You go to the hospital and see mom in critical condition, but all you can think about is yourself. I can't stand your pity-party.

Don't give me this crap about you had to leave because mom was ignoring you to get back at you. That's nonsense. Where do you get off saying that?

I'm your sister. The one who was always there for you. I'm not the others who didn't like having you there. I defended you. I protected you when no one else cared. I know...our other sisters showed up...and that's why you left. It

238

wasn't mom. They didn't say a word to you, so how could they put you down this time?

So now you run away AGAIN! I can't even talk to you about it because you disappeared all day and slipped into your room long after everyone was in bed. Well, guess what? I heard you come in and sneak into the room I so nicely made up for you. You're so welcome.

We will talk about this...face to face...before you run back to Washington,

Infuriated Rebecca

Sheila,

I really miss you and Washington. I've only been in Kansas City one day and it's a complete disaster. My sister just left a nasty letter in my bedroom. It's the nastiest letter she's ever written. I feel like dirt, just as I did my whole life. This confirms I made to right choice in moving.

I couldn't handle seeing my mom dying in a hospital bed. Now I'm supposed to feel like a villain for leaving the hospital and trying to sort things out alone. This is why I didn't want you to come. You don't need all this stress.

At the same time, I really wish you were here. I've never desired holding you so much. This room is so lonely, not only from your absence, but the lack of support in this God-forsaken city. No one needs this kind of stress in their life.

Anyway…That brings me to my next argument. Rebecca, that woman who gave birth to me, and my other sisters, claim to be Christians. What's the point in serving a God if it turns you into a critical, finger pointing idiot? None of them are perfect, but they sure think so.

I hate to dump all this on you after another grueling night of serving drunks. I wish I had some good news. Please write me at my sister's address so I know you're alive.

I love you,

Rich

Overbearing Rebecca,

I want you to understand all I'm going through right now. There's a million thoughts going on in my head. I don't know what to do with all this.

I know you've always been supportive of me and I appreciate that. Even though I left for Washington State, mad at you and the rest of the world, you have to understand why I left. You may think you know the whole story, but you really don't. It's impossible to explain my struggles to someone who doesn't listen.

I haven't left yet. You just assume I'm heading back home because I ran from the hospital. You're wrong. Believe it or not, sometimes you **are** wrong. I needed to sort things out. I'm still here.

Of course, you want me to see mom again. I just don't see the point. She can't hear me or see me. That's nothing new. She's never treated me like I was worth her time. The only difference this time is she's in a stroke-induced coma. Finally, she has an excuse.

What am I supposed to do with all this baggage she caused? I want to be able to focus on her condition, but it's a real struggle. If you're as Christian as you say, try to put yourself in my shoes for a minute. Dig inside yourself and

LETTERS FROM SECLUSION

pretend you were the one of 5 children mom gave up for adoption.

Enough said,

Rich

Stubborn brother, Rich,

I read the letter you left for me this morning. I prayed a lot...then pondered. I shouldn't have snapped at you. It's hard seeing mom in the hospital after all these years. I get it. This is a taxing time for us all.

I'm hoping you will come back to the house so we can talk about this like civilized human beings. I'm glad you came, as difficult as it may be.

No, you don't have to think of her as your mother, if you so choose. As much as I hate to admit it, she didn't play that role in your life. I will never understand her attitude toward you. You don't deserve it.

Do me a favor and don't let her actions make you push me away. I'm hoping you and I can start a new relationship. Can we forget the past? I want you to get to know my husband and kids. I've said this before and I hope it will sink in this time.

Visiting hours at the hospital start at 10 a.m. I hope to see you there. I don't know if mom will wake up or not, but you have a family who needs you right now. You asked me to look inside myself. Now I'm asking you to do the same.

I need you, now, more than ever,

Rebecca

Ranting Rebecca,

I'm hearing you. My concern is how the other 3 siblings will treat me. You know how they always push me away and say nasty things to me. It will be 100 times worse now. I'd rather not go when they're around.

I went to the library today and researched stroke. The outlook isn't good for her. The same thought keeps going through my mind…she will die and won't know I made the effort to see her. What am I supposed to do with that?

I'm stuck here. This hurts so much, I feel like someone stabbed me in the gut. Tears are actually filling my eyes. I haven't cried since I broke up with Cynthia, when I was 19. I felt like an idiot then, as I do now.

I will go to see mom again, even though I don't want to see certain people. You're my big sister…and as far as I'm concerned, you're my only sister.

See you at the hospital,

Rich

Little brother, Rich,

Seeing you walk into that hospital room today, was awkward, but brought back some good times. I know I picked on you as a kid, but that's what big sisters do. I never wanted you to move away. I won't lecture you about it. I'm sure you've gotten an earful from others.

As good as it was to see you, it was heartbreaking seeing you unhappy. I miss that smile you used to have when I watched you and Rebecca spend time together. You two used to laugh all the time.

In all honesty, it made me jealous. That's why I teased you all the time. I was young and didn't think about how it made you feel. Kids do that...especially teenagers.

I hope you can forgive me. Life is very different without you. Every time the family gets together, even in a really crowded room, it seems empty.

I don't know what else to say, but I'm sorry. Please be a part of our lives again. Once mom is gone, we will only have each other.

Don't let the past ruin that,

Danielle

FORGIVENESS IS A CHOICE

Rich,

Thank you for showing up at 10am, like I asked. I told you no one would mistreat you. Everyone misses their little brother. Even though the older 3 did nasty things to you, they always loved you.

We were shocked when you left. We cried once we realized you made an effort not to be found. You told your best friend, Kelly, but not your family. It hurt deeply.

I know I'm lecturing you again, but it's worth repeating. I just want you to remember God is in control of **all** things. Running away doesn't fix things, only God can. He's the King who sits on the throne.

It wasn't by accident that you came back here. The Holy Spirit was working on you from the moment you left. It may not have felt that

LETTERS FROM SECLUSION

way, but He was there to guide you thought it.

The decisions you made weren't in His plan for your life. That's a given. The truth is, God is so powerful that He can take the tragedies in our lives and use them for our good. Those hardships strengthen us and transform us into a stronger person.

You may still believe there is no God and rolling your eyes right now. That doesn't matter. The truth is still truth. The Bible is the true and infallible Word of God. All of our questions are answered in the Word. If He can part the Red Sea, sparing the lives of the Israelites from certain death, then He can heal you from your circumstances.

I wanted to tell you this and that I still am proud of you. This is all hard on you, but now you're fighting, with His help.

There's someone who really wants to see you again. It's not a family member, but someone really close to you. The only person you told where you were going. Yes, Kelly is anxious to see your face again.

Good friends are hard to come by. I praise God for Kelly, who was bold enough to tell mom where you went. I know it made you mad when you got that first letter from mom, but it was all in the Lord's divine plan.

I don't know how all this is going to work out with you living in Washington, but I don't need to know...that's God's job. It's our job to continue to pray.

I've talked enough, but I want to encourage you to meet with Kelly. There's a reason for this all. Trust

me, and more importantly, know
you are loved.

Trust and obey,

Faithful Rebecca

Cutie-Pie Rich,

I've missed you these last few days. The tavern hasn't changed, with the exception of your absence. I keep looking at your seat that faces the bar. It's either been empty or has someone else sitting there.

Then I go home to that crazy college girl. She's always obnoxious with her parties or whatever she's doing in her bedroom. After leaving that loud bar scene every night, I really wish I could go home to a quiet environment.

Then during the day, I can't see you, like I normally do. It makes the days long. I know it's been less than a week, but it doesn't seem like it. I wish you would come home.

I'm sorry your family has proven to be the same, nasty people you remembered. I've always said, people don't change. That's what you get with all those church going, Bible thumping hypocrites. It doesn't surprise me they mistreat you.

It makes me mad though. Dating you has proven to me how caring and warm a person can be. I never thought I would find such a

LETTERS FROM SECLUSION

wonderful man. You don't deserve to be treated like an insignificant outsider.

It's torture knowing you're so far,

Sheila

Rebecca,

As soon as I read Kelly's name in your last letter, my heart leapt in my throat. Am I really ready to meet with anyone else right now? My stomach is in knots, just thinking about it. I don't want to sound like a chicken…I think I see some feathers forming on my legs. I'll be clucking in no time.

As for your comment about me rolling my eyes, you have no idea what I was thinking or doing, thank you very much. Actually, I've been thinking about this relationship you have with God. I don't know if it's real or just something to hold on to. It's hard to grasp my mind around it.

How does anyone know that God has everything planned out from the beginning of time? What if everything happens by chance? That's what Darwinism is all about. I'm not claiming to believe we evolved from primates, only because some scientists now say our molecular structure doesn't match. Also, if we evolved from monkeys, apes, or whatever, why do we co-exist? Now, I'm evolving from a chicken into an orangutan.

I have too much on my mind. I feel like a teenager again. Sweat is pouring from my forehead from all the stress.

Life is too short for all this. Part of me wants to go back home and forget it all. I miss Sheila.

I'll consider meeting with Kelly,

Beleaguered Rich

Rich, my love,

It's been a week since I wrote and you haven't responded. That bothers me. I have no idea if you're ok or what's going on. A girl needs to know if her boyfriend is still alive. It's like you're shutting me out like you've done your family.

I understand why you don't want them in your life. My fear is, now that you're there, they are corrupting you against me. Toxic people love to run their mouths.

Please let me know what's going on. I need you in my life. There's no one who can love me the way you do.

If I don't hear from you soon, I will make the trip to see you,

Upset Sheila

Mom,

This is my first attempt to respond to any of your letters. To say the least, it's awkward. I know I left without saying goodbye, but I had good reasons. There's no getting around it, your decisions with me left a lot to be desired.

It may be a waste of time writing you at all, since you're still in a coma. I wish I knew if you will ever wake up. The doctors around here haven't changed much at this hospital. They don't know anything about your condition. They tell me the same things I have read on the internet. They probably did the same. It's amazing how incompetent a person can be after years of schooling and residency.

I almost trashed this letter. There's no way of knowing if you will ever read it. If there's a God above, part of me wants Him to bring you out of this coma so you can see I made the effort to see you.

I'll never understand why you put me up for adoption after keeping 4 other children. Was I that bad of a person? I was only a baby. You didn't even give me a chance. What's wrong with you? What's wrong with me?

FORGIVENESS IS A CHOICE

I went from home to home, being nothing but rejected by everyone. I wish you knew how it feels to be booted by your own mother and sisters, then by every foster home and center where you've been assigned.

The real kicker is you acting like you're the superior parent because my father isn't in my life. It's obvious neither of you deserve the title "Superior Parent." To top it off, you try to shove your "God" down my throat. What kind of god would accept you throwing your only son in the garbage?

Wasn't it God that sent His one and only Son to save the world? That's what it says in John 3:16. Yes, I've read some of my Bible. It's been a lot of years since I dusted it off and put it to use. I'm still not sure how true the scriptures are, but I'm giving it a try. No promises.

Here's to the hopes of you waking,

Rich

Kelly,

I'm not sure how you feel about seeing me again. My sister told me you can't wait to see me, but I'm not sure if I can believe everything she says. Sometimes she tells me things out of manipulation. If you're okay with it, I would love to see you.

I know you and I have our ups and downs in our friendship, but I'm glad you've remained loyal. That word, loyalty, is more valuable than words. No one knows what it means anymore. I'm glad you're in my life.

This is really awkward to say, but I started reading my Bible again. Everyone back home is a Christian and talks to me about Jesus. I'm not sure what to think about it. I just wanted to let you know.

My mind is a jumbled up mess. This stuff with mom, my sisters, thoughts of you, and my relationship with Sheila, my girlfriend in Washington. I feel like I'm going insane sometimes.

I'm not making much sense,

Perplexed Rich

Sheila,

Okay…it's late at night and I finally have time alone. I'm sorry it's taken me this long to write. I've had a hard week. All the difficult feelings I had years ago, when I moved away, came back. I have to say, though, after a few days of hiding in my turtle shell, my emotions calmed and I was able to look at things objectively.

I have a responsibility to my family. I know they haven't always been the most supportive, but they still are my family…half-blooded, but that's not my fault or theirs. Speaking of being supportive, that's what my siblings need from me right now.

Don't make the trip out here. There's no point in traveling all this way. As much as I'd love to see you, it's not practical. You have to work and flights are expensive. I'll be home before you know it. The first thing I'm going to do is hold you.

Don't worry, I haven't forgotten you,

Rich

My Good Friend Rich,

Of course, I want to see you.
When I heard you were back in
town, my heart rejoiced. The real
question is: where should I meet
you? I know you've been spending
a lot of time in the hospital, so
I know it's hard to find time.
There's no doubt you are exhausted
when you leave in the evenings.

Just as I thought you forgot about
me or were mad at me, you pop into
my life again. My work schedule
is a mess this week, but I'll make
the time for you.

I'd love to talk to you about the
Lord and anything else you want to
discuss. Let's make it a date
soon.

Promise me you won't go back to
Washington without seeing me,

Kelly

Rich,

I asked you to meet me in mom's room right at 10am for a reason. I asked everyone else to stay away for a couple hours, so we can visit with mom alone. It may seem strange to say "meet" when mom isn't awake, but...well you'll see when you arrive this morning.

I didn't arrange for a huge party or anything. We need some quiet time. It's been a lot of years since I've had the chance to hang out with you alone...little brother.

See you soon,

Rebecca

LETTERS FROM SECLUSION

Critical Rebecca,

The last time I saw you alone, we had a big fight. I hope that doesn't happen again. What do you have planned? I can't take any more adversity. My heart is beating fast, just thinking about it. I'll wait with my mouth shut and try not to roll my eyes.

I'm tempted to pray about it, like you always talk about. Chances are, I'm speaking to the air anyway, so why bother? I watched that Christian network last night on TV. It was interesting to see so many people excited for God. I didn't know whether I should laugh or take it serious.

Millions of people believe in God and others are adamantly against Christianity. Even within Christian circles, people can't agree on what the scriptures mean. How does one know what's right? What if all the ideas about what the Bible teaches somehow fits together? Is there a possibility everyone is wasting their time with religious beliefs?

I don't mean to boggle your mind with a bunch of questions so early in the morning. I see mom is sleeping, but in a different position. Did the nurse move her?

There I go with the questions again,

Rich

Silly Rich,

You make me laugh. God isn't afraid of your questions and neither am I. There is only one God and the Bible is true and infallible. I've mentioned this before. As far as who is right, you really need to get into a Bible based church and start fellowshipping with safe men.

I would love it if you'd come to my church this Sunday. There's a men's group that would love to have you. I'll introduce you to some of the guys my husband knows.

Anyway, as nice as it is to chat with you, I want you to see something. When you come back from the snack machine (you always loved Butterfingers), I want you to take a good look at mom's bed.

I'll step out,

Rebecca

FORGIVENESS IS A CHOICE

Mom,

You're awake! I'm not sure if you can hear me, but I see you looking at me for the first time in many years. It looks as if you shriveled down to nothing. Age has not been good to you.

I don't want to sound harsh…I don't know if I want to be harsh. This is really weird seeing you, especially in a hospital bed. I was so angry when we spoke last that I didn't even say goodbye.

It's impossible to know what you're thinking if you don't talk to me. I'm gibber-jabbing like there is no tomorrow while you say nothing. Are you able to talk?

I can't say I'm hurt right now. I honestly can't describe what I'm feeling. I've buried my thoughts and emotions for far too long. Now I'm asking myself: Why? What purpose did it serve?

You haven't even given me a smile or a nod. It makes me believe you don't know I'm here. Perhaps you don't want me here. There was a part of me that thought you wanted to see me once more before you passed away. I guess I was wrong.

We can talk when you're ready,

Rich

Dear Brother Rich,

Don't leave yet. I was standing outside the door, listening to you talk to mom. I don't mean to get emotional, but you really don't understand how much she loves you.

Mom isn't ignoring you. The doctor said she can only open her eyes at this point. It is possible she will recover fully, but there's only a slim chance. She can't talk, feed herself, or even go to the bathroom without a catheter. Yes, she woke up, but her chances of living through this is next to impossible. It's going to take continuous prayer.

Now for the real reason I wanted you here alone. There's someone who really wants to see you. I'm sure you know who. Please don't leave.

FORGIVENESS IS A CHOICE

I'm going to have to trust that you will listen to me for the first time in your life. All I can do is sit here, toward the back of the room and wait.

Please stay,

Rebecca

Kelly,

I was surprised to see you come in to mom's room. I looked over at Rebecca who is smiling as wide as she can. I know you two planned this whole thing. I'm pleased you took time away from your work day to visit me.

Seeing you standing there brings back lots of good memories. I think you're more beautiful now than ever. Your flowing dark hair and bright blue eyes reminds me of the first time I saw you in high heels. Between the dress you wore that night and your precious smile, I don't know what was more stunning.

I don't know what to say at this point. I suppose you want to see my mother. She's in bad shape. Apparently, this is the end…or close to it.

You're another one who doesn't know what to say to me after all these years. In letters, you bluntly let me know what you're thinking. It's too quiet in here. I'm surrounded by 3 women and no one has said a word but me.

What are the odds of that happening?

Awkward Rich

Sweet-Talking Rich,

Thanks for the kind words. It's nice to finally know you think I'm beautiful. Sorry I didn't respond right away, but you shocked me. I'm flattered. Just for the record, I've always found you extremely attractive.

I wish the circumstances were different. I don't like talking about this in front of your sister and mother. It's a little embarrassing. Now that I said that, Rebecca volunteered to leave. Isn't she the best sister in the world? You're richly blessed.

I'm sorry things are bad with your mom. As you know, I knew her a long time. It will be hard on me as well. She always welcomed me as part of the family.

So…from here, what should we do? I have to get to work, but I want to see you later. What are your plans this evening?

I don't want to be too forward,

Kelly

LETTERS FROM SECLUSION

Rebecca,

You can come back now. Seeing you walk in here with that little grin makes me want to smack you...but I won't. You knew Kelly was attracted to me all these years, didn't you? You know I have a girlfriend, who's mad at me because I haven't talked to her much this week.

I remember when you tried to tell me all my girlfriends were no good. Now you bring Kelly here dressed in her best with full makeup. I should be mad at you, but seeing her again was like a medicine. She clearly takes good care of herself.

I guess I have some decisions to make. Sheila is so beautiful and caring. I miss seeing her and laughing with her. She makes me feel like a man should.

Then again, Kelly has been there for me all these years, no matter how difficult I am at times. She's patient and always gentle with me. I've told her that more than once. I pause as I say this... I've always found her attractive, but we were good friends...that's all.

I never thought she would see me as a boyfriend. I'm still not sure. If I tell her how I feel, it could ruin our friendship. It's not worth that. It's also not fair to Sheila. She deserves my faithfulness.

Anyway, enough about my girl problems. As a Christian, how should you respond to mom's condition? Is talking to God all we have left? What if He wants her to die because she will be better off?

If she does pass, I would have missed the last few years of her life. I'm sure you realize that and have a hard time keeping your mouth shut about it. Sometimes I think it was for the best, and other times, I think I could have handled it better.

How many people experience what I've been through? I'm scratching my head, hoping for the answers to jump out at me. That's stupid.

Not to leave you on a sour note, but I'm going to head back to your place,

Rich

Infuriating Rich,

I'm trying to be patient and understand what you're going through, but it gets a little tiresome to hear you mulling over the same things. When are you going to except the things that happened? Life comes at you in all directions. No one can explain it. You can't either. I have to agree with you on one thing: It's stupid to talk about it over and over.

Yes, I have thought about how much you've missed. Washington State may seem like the right place for you, but you're wrong. It may only be my opinion, but you have a life here in Kansas City.

The big question is: what is holding you back? You've mentioned your work is thinning out, so that can't be worth going back to. There's Sheila, which I don't like the idea of you dating. What made you think a bartender was someone who'd make a good wife? She's too young for you anyway. It looks like she just graduated college. What were you thinking?

The only thing I can see holding you to Washington is your house. You really made a rash move buying a house there when you didn't know if you would like it there. Most people rent for a while until they decide it's somewhere they want to stay for 20 years or more. You threatened to slap me...I should slap you, little bro.

I know you like Kelly and were too shy to tell her. What is it going to take for you to understand she adores you? Don't think for one second that she will reject your offer of a relationship.

I know you feel rejected by many people, but don't let that stop you from following your heart. Use the wisdom God gave you and tell Kelly how you feel. She's waiting to hear more from you than "I think you're beautiful." There are millions of beautiful women out there. She wants to know what makes her special to you.

I'm hoping you left the hospital to go see Kelly,

Rebecca

Kelly,

It wasn't easy to get away from the hospital. You know how my family controls me, if I allow them. My sister reamed me out about another girlfriend. You don't need to hear all this again. You've heard enough of my complaining through the years.

I hope this restaurant is to your liking. I've never eaten here, so it will be an experience for us both. The Capital Grill is supposed to be one of the best fine dining restaurants in Kansas City. I checked out several of them and I'm hoping this one will give us a memorable experience.

I'm not going to talk your ear off tonight, like I always do. I want to hear all about your life since I've been gone. I'm sure many things have happened that we haven't discussed. All my letters have been solely about me and my struggles. It's your turn to talk.

I just realized how selfish I've been. All those years I've hidden myself away from the world…or I should say, my old world, and found a new one. I work all day at home, and then spend all evening getting drunk. No wonder my sister doesn't like my dating a bartender.

LETTERS FROM SECLUSION

It's lovely to see you in your elegant clothes. I miss your smile. I don't know what I was thinking when I chose to run away. You were there for me all the time and I was too pig headed to see it.

I'm glad you came,

Rich

Rich,

I can't tell you how nice it is to see your handsome face. I prayed all these years that you would come back. With tears in my eyes, I praise Him. I know it's only for a visit and I accept that. Maybe I can convince you to stay.

Don't beat yourself up about leaving Kansas City. You were upset and deeply hurt. I understand how embarrassing it must have been when Rebecca saw you passed out on your living room floor. The first thing you thought to do was run and hide.

It's in the past and now it's time to forgive yourself. God forgives you and I do too. Believe it or not, Rebecca forgives you. I know she has a harsh way about her, but don't mistake that for hatred. She loves you more than you know and was deeply hurt when you left.

Your mother's stroke is what brought you here. I get that. This may shock you a little, but it was a blessing in disguise. I'm not saying God made her have a stroke to prompt you to come, but He draws blessings out of every tragedy.

Even though you ran from your family and friends, and from God, He still loved you the same. His healing hand was on you while you went through all your struggles. When you were sitting in that bar every night, He looked down on you in sadness, but believe it or not, He had a plan. When you're at your house, all alone, searching for a place where you belong, He's there.

I know there are times you feel like God doesn't care.

I've heard people say God created us and left us to fend for ourselves. That's nonsense. He has a plan for your life. From the beginning of your life, He knew you would move away. He also knew you would come back, sit at this table with me, and have this conversation.

I know you're dating another woman in Washington. This isn't going to be something you're going to like, but I agree with your sister. Considering your past struggles with alcohol, it's probably better that you not date a bartender. Think about it…you wouldn't have met her if you didn't go into that place. I can't believe she's part of God's plan.

I'm not saying that because of the way I feel about you. I want you to be happy and part of that is seeing you in a healthy relationship.

I'd like to think you would love me the way I love you. I've always loved you Rich. I know I kept it at friendship, because you never gave me the impression you were interested in me. I can remember all the times you talked about other girls you liked. I cringed every time I saw you gawk at someone else. I never said anything, but it broke my heart.

I'm only going to ask you once. I know I'm nothing special. Sheila fills that role in your life. As much as it hurts to think of you with her, if I don't tell you how I feel this time, there won't be another opportunity...I'm sure of that. I'm asking you to love me...and love the Lord.

By now, you should see the unconditional love I have for you. Sometimes you infuriate me with your stubbornness, negative attitude about the world, and all your anger toward Christians. Right now, none of that matters. I love you anyway, just as I always have.

You didn't have to take me to an expensive restaurant to impress me. I would be fine with fast food. I'm interested in spending time with you, not in what kind of restaurant you can afford. It's beautiful in here with the African mahogany paneling and the elaborate chandeliers. I'm flattered you wanted to share the memory with me.

Since you're paying, I'm gonna have prosciutto wrapped mozzarella and the filet mignon. Nothing is cheap on the menu. I'm not used to

282

being spoiled by a man or anyone else...not like this.

You're a sweet guy,

Kelly

Blue Eyed Kelly,

Don't worry how much things cost. I wanted to treat you to a nice restaurant. Besides, I knew you liked filet mignon. It doesn't surprise me you ordered it. You know I'm fine with a Caesar salad and the lamb. My stomach would be growling if I wasn't so nervous.

Okay…enough about food. I thought the man was supposed to confess his love to the woman, not the other way around. I admit I love you too. My feelings are so strong…look at me, I'm shaking. I don't know if I can eat with my stomach in knots. I'm acting like a teenager. I'm a sad case.

As for Sheila, don't worry about her. I haven't talked to her much since I've been here. My mind has been preoccupied, not only with mom and family, but with anticipation of seeing you again.

It's interesting that you point out my faults at the same time you tell me you love me. I guess, there must be a reason you're here.

I've only heard of unconditional love from the Bible. I didn't think it was possible between people. I'm learning lots since I've been back.

I have been pondering the Bible and if Jesus really died for us. I found myself praying for my mom over the last few days. I even asked if God could hear me. I felt silly talking to the air.

I know you want me to love the Lord, but it's been so long since I've gone to church or read the Bible. It feels weird. I would have to learn the scriptures again.

If it wasn't for mom taking us to church and forcing me to go to Sunday school, I wouldn't have gone. Most of my foster parents didn't go to church. I certainly didn't get to church while I stayed at the foster home. No one made me go, so I stayed in bed until noon, and then played in the yard most of the day.

I love looking at your eyes. I never realized how much I missed you. I'm trying not to criticize myself too much, but I really thought I found a place where I belonged, in Washington. I was a fool.

Life is falling apart there. My job, where I was overloaded with work, is starting to thin out. Projects are being cancelled and my paychecks are starting to diminish down to nothing. Well…I can't say nothing. I still make more in a month than most people earn all year. Not to brag…it's just the truth.

There's an old man I thought was a good mentor for me. I met him at the tavern where Sheila works. He gave me insight that made sense. We have similar backgrounds and have the same struggles with betrayal.

I thought I found a good friend. He encouraged me to pursue Sheila after all his talk about not trusting anyone. He'd say, "People always use you and stab you in the back in the end." Then he told me, "You never know when love comes your way."

So, I started talking to Sheila because he pressured me into it. We liked each other and started dating. When I told the old man about it, he got jealous and stopped talking to me. Apparently, he betrays people like he accuses others of doing.

I guess, I'm saying things aren't as good as I thought they were. My Washington world is falling apart, except for Sheila. I thought she was my whole world. Now I'm not sure.

A correction is in order. You are special to me. I came back and took the time to go on our first date. It's long overdue. I don't know what I was thinking all those years when I could have been loving you.

Our food is here…enjoy,

Rich

Painting The Town Rich,

I couldn't wait for you to come home, so I wrote instead. How did your date go with Kelly? I'm so anxious to hear your answer. You know I like to nose in your business because you're my brother.

There were too many years I didn't get to see you. It was hard, but I managed to wait until the weekends. That's why it hurt so much when you moved away without even saying goodbye. I finally had you full time and you got involved with toxic things and poof...you were out of my life again. I hate to bring it up again, but it still hurts.

I didn't fix you up with Kelly just to prompt you to move to Kansas City again. I do have to say, however, that I really like her for you. She's always loved you and cared for the

288

real you. No one knows you as well as Kelly. You know that as well as the rest of us. There were times she should have smacked you on the floor, but it's not her way. She's very gentle.

I won't get to see you come in. You two are out awfully late. I'll take that as a good thing. I hope you got to express your true feelings and didn't hold anything back. Go for it!

I'm yawning. It's time to hit the sack. I'll talk to you tomorrow...whether you like it or not, little bro!

I love you,

Rebecca

Mom,

I see you sleeping this morning. It's about 10:30. Everyone has to work, so I'm here alone. There's much we need to talk about. I'm hoping you will open your eyes soon, so I can at least know you're listening.

It's stupid sitting here talking to myself. What else do I have to do? I guess I'll write instead. You've been waiting for me to answer your plethora of letters. Here it goes.

Looking around this hospital room, the smells and the sound of the dripping faucet, all bring back a long history of uncertainty. I don't know if that's the right word, but I never had the feeling of home. At least, in the hospital I knew I was being taken care of.

I was in this hospital many times as a kid. Most of the time it was trips to the ER because I was a klutz. If it wasn't you, it was some stranger bringing me. I'll never forget the time I fell out of the tree and broke my arm. Mrs. Campbell, one of my foster parents, didn't care about me. She kept telling me how much of an inconvenience it was for her to leave work and rush me to the hospital.

Obviously, I was a burden to her, rather than being that person who wanted to nurture me and raise me into a man. I felt guilty for falling on a tree root and fracturing both my radius and ulna. The pain wasn't enough. She had to call me a brat to make things worse.

I admit, it wouldn't have happened if I wasn't being a peeping Tom. I was checking out that cute blonde who lived next door. She smiled at me once, but never talked to me. I was too shy to approach her. That's the reason I climbed the tree to see her. I hope she never found out. I'm still embarrassed thinking about it.

I know I keep going over my past. Rebecca keeps telling me to "get over it." I hate that phrase. It makes me think no one cares or even tries to understand what I've been through. I've tried to get past all the unbearable pain, to no avail.

I always end up in a bar somewhere, getting smashed. It's the only way I can laugh and enjoy myself. I know it's a medication, but it works. I've learned when the margarita glass is empty, the problem is still there. Then I order another and another. It's a vicious cycle I can't correct. It feels good when I've had too many.

This is the first time I've cried aloud in years…probably since I was a kid. I don't know if I'm sad or angry. It's probably a mixture. I often wondered if anyone else has gone through this. Am I alone? Am I just a reject?

Mom…why did you ditch me? You had 4 other children and you kept them all. Is it because I was a boy? Was I a burden to you? I felt like trash. I still do.

All these years I convinced myself no one wanted me around. I ran away and found a new life in Washington. Now that's proven to be a bust. Sure, I made lots of money there, but I made the same here in Kansas City, in fewer hours. You pushed me away with your snotty attitude toward me.

This is your fault. It's not mine. You did this.

All the gifts you gave me were nice. I enjoyed the weekends away from my foster home too. If it wasn't for my weekend passes, I wouldn't have gotten to know Rebecca. We're closer than I will ever be to my other 3 sisters. It may sound cold to you, but none of that makes up for what you've done.

I can hardly breathe through my tears. My stomach is in knots. I wish you could see what you've done to me. What kind of mother abandons their child? I guess if my father, whoever he is, can do it, so can you.

292

Now I'm being asked to leave for making too much noise. My crying is disturbing other patients. So, I'll leave this letter with you.

Enjoy your rest,

Distressed and Embarrassed Rich

Rebecca,

I got a plane ticket to head back to Washington. I can't take any more of this. I'm getting physically sick from it all. I really didn't want to face anyone and bring up my past realities. Now that it's all surfaced again, I just want to go home.

I'm sure you're going to say I'm acting like a baby. Have fun. Go gossip to your sisters about it. At least I won't have to hear it. When you see me at your place tonight, I don't want to get into an argument. The only thing I need from you is a little understanding, not chastisement.

I know you want to hear about my date with Kelly. It was wonderful and I will miss her, but my life isn't here anymore. I don't belong here. I'm hoping you will tell her for me. It will be too hard to face her again, just to tell her I can't be with her.

I know this hurts you too. I'm sorry…I really am. I need time to think things over. I have no life here or in Washington. What am I supposed to do? I'm hitting the bars as soon as they open.

Don't try to stop me,

Rich

Withdrawing Rich,

I saw you go into that bar this afternoon, way before dinner time. I figured you went to see mom alone and it was too much for you. When are you going to learn that alcohol won't cure you?

I know you don't want a lecture and I won't give you one. I'll keep my mouth shut about it. There is something you need to see though. I want you to stay a few more days, if it's possible. I know you have to get back to work.

Mom would like to see you. She was awake when I got there this afternoon, after work. She was disappointed you weren't there. She did, however, read both your letters. Yes, she's able to read and comprehend what you wrote.

FORGIVENESS IS A CHOICE

It appears the prayer chain is working. She's much better today than just 24 hours ago. She's not talking, only a few words here and there. It's hard to understand her, but even the doctors are shocked at her progress.

God hears our prayers. It may not be something you think is real, but it's working. The church, people at work, and throughout our family and friends are believing mom will fully recover. When the doctors say nothing can be done, God says, yes there is! He's the great physician who heals beyond human capacity.

Enough of my ranting. Please don't go. Everyone needs you. Mom needs you, Kelly needs you, and I need you. Give it one more day.

Do it for your sister,

Rebecca

Kelly,

It's 5 o'clock in the morning and I can't sleep. I had to write you. Rebecca has me bugged. I was gonna sneak out of town, back to Washington…again. I decided to stay another day or two. If, for no other reason, to see you again. Maybe it's best if you swing by the hospital after work.

There's something I need to talk to you about. I don't want to say it in a letter. I'm going through a hard time…even harder than usual. It'll make more sense to you when I see you.

Thanks for the nice evening the other night. You are truly a wonderful woman. I'll never go to fine dining again. It fit my budget but not my liking. I don't understand why anyone would pay $50 or more for an entrée that's not even the size of my fist. We got a big laugh at leaving there and grabbing a pizza afterwards.

I can't wait to see you again. The hours will go slowly, for sure.

I love you,

Insomniac Rich

Rich,

My wonderful son. Rebecca is writing this as I dictate because my hands don't work like they should. I'm having a hard time figuring out what to say after all these years. It was hard to read your 2 letters. They showed anger, sadness, and you even seem hopeless.

I don't want you to feel that way. I know there's nothing I can say that will fix everything you've experienced. Things happen to us all, but not to the magnitude of your pain. Don't hear me saying I can understand what I put you through…and I know it was my doing…just know putting you up for adoption was the hardest decision I had to make.

I was young and inexperienced in life. I had 4 girls almost back to back. It was overwhelming. When you came along, I had 3 kids in diapers. There was no man to help me and I was too prideful to ask for help from your grandmother. These are lame excuses, and I can't say I did what was best for you. I took the easy way out.

So you ask, why? I hated your father. He charmed me into the bedroom and I fell for him...hard. He was handsome and knew how to entice me. I didn't have a husband and the nights were long. My busy days were short compared to the nights.

I cried silently through the night too many times. I prayed for the right man to come along. I waited and praised God for the blessing of 4 girls. All along, I felt empty. I knew something was missing and I thought your father was the answer.

I was young and didn't understand the concept of pheromones.

It lasted a few months and you were conceived. All the prayers I made for a good man ended in moral turpitude. It was my choice as well as his. Your father found another young woman to charm and he ran off with her. I found out it was only a pattern with him. He didn't care about much...certainly not me...and not you.

I know I've been harsh to you and even cold. It's because the older you got, the more you reminded me of that father of yours. He'll never be a man. Real men honor their responsibilities, including their children. I can only wonder how many he has with other women.

I shouldn't dump all this on you. It was my mess up and I have to own up to it. You're right, I can't make up for the hurt I caused you. I could always say your foster parents and foster care center weren't something I can control. That is true, but if I had kept you, you wouldn't have experienced it.

I'm a bad mom. I'm sure that's what you want to hear. So, I said it. I'm not being sarcastic. I made terrible mistakes. When you come, and I hope I see you soon, we can talk more about this.

All I ask is that you love me though all this. That's what Jesus would want you to do. He wiped away our sins when He hung on the cross and the only way to receive that forgiveness is to forgive those who hurt you. It says so in Mark 11:26 and Matthew 6:14-15. Both of us have healing to do. I'm sure you can agree on that.

FORGIVENESS IS A CHOICE

I'm hoping you take the time to read this entire letter. I need you to as much as you need to hear it. Believe it or not, I really do love you.

I can't wait to see you,

Mom

Ailing Mom,

I took your letter from Rebecca. It was an awkward feeling seeing you awake finally, only to see my sister present your letter. Apparently, you can't give it to me. It makes me bitter to think, after all these years, now you want to talk.

Regardless, I read it and was shocked by the content. I thought you were going to have harsh things to say, but I was wrong. It was good to hear you open up and admit your mistakes. I always thought a woman didn't have the integrity to admit when they were wrong.

I have a real problem with you asking me to love you through this. I didn't get any of that when I needed it from you. I know I've said this before, but I keep hearing the same voice in my head, "You just need to get over it." I wish I had a dime every time I heard that from you or my sisters. I'd be able to buy the moon.

I'm not sure I want to talk about this with you. It's been so long and we've gotten nowhere in the past. What's all this about "God?" You were a Christian all those years while you were making multiple babies. It makes me wonder how many men you slept with. How many fathers are there?

Is being alone so hard that you had to have a man...any man? I didn't have a woman for years and I was fine with it. I didn't think I was half a person without someone to love.

I'll admit, Sheila has made me feel alive again. She's sweet and has a good heart. Most importantly, she accepts me for who I am. I don't have to change anything about myself to please her. We got along well from the start. It's refreshing to have her in my life.

I know this all seems weird after getting back in touch with Kelly. She's a special lady and I think the world of her. I never knew she was in love with me from the start. I was oblivious to it. She's beautiful and has always been loyal to me.

It was nice to take her to that fancy restaurant and talk everything out. There was chemistry there years ago and I didn't know it. I liked her, but was too afraid to say. I didn't want it to mess up the good friendship we had. Now I wonder if it was all wasted time.

I guess the answer to that is easy. We loved each other and didn't admit it. How different would life be if we dated in high school? I wouldn't have gotten involved with all those crazy girls. I'm, apparently, not the greatest at picking the right ladies.

LETTERS FROM SECLUSION

Back to the subject of you and me. I will do my best to forgive and move on. It's just hard to think about letting you off the hook, like nothing happened. I don't like talking about this, since it brings up so much hurt. I'm glad I'm sitting on a park bench while writing this. I wouldn't want to cause another scene at the hospital with my crying.

I feel like a baby who needs to scream for comfort. As usual, there's no one around to help me heal. The park is empty in the middle of the day. I hope joggers don't come by. That would be embarrassing.

Okay…I just got back from a long walk around the lake. It's peaceful here, even with the traffic whirling by.

I still ponder the possibility of God. Everyone needs somewhere to turn. It's therapeutic, if that's what works for you. I just don't know if I'm ready to accept the lifestyle change the Bible talks about. Can I really stop drinking and medicate my pain with church?

Even if I start going to church again, what happens after I walk out the church doors? I can't believe everyone who goes to church is as happy as they appear on Sunday morning. It's almost like the pastor has programmed a bunch of robots. How many fake people walk through the church doors every week…faithfully?

My thoughts about other people isn't helping me heal, I know. If I have any integrity at all, I must say, I have a problem with alcohol. Isn't there more to life than what I've been getting?

I don't know what to do. Everywhere I turn, there's adversity. Some of it is my fault.

I'll see you in a little while,

Down in the dumps Rich

My son, Rich,

It was good to see you walk in this afternoon. I was wondering if you were going to visit me today. It does my heart good that you are making an effort to work on our relationship.

I'm feeling a little worse today. I can't move my hands still, plus I can't make my mouth work to talk. It's frustrating after being able to say a few words yesterday. Forget my legs. The doctor came in this morning and told me I will never walk again. I'm believing for a supernatural healing.

As for you. Don't spend too much time thinking about all your woes. It will depress you. It's no wonder you were crying at the park. I'm sorry you had to go through that alone. When you're down, you should have someone with you who can help with emotional support.

I know you're confused about all the ladies in your life. Most men should be so lucky to have two beautiful women who desire them. You know we're all pulling for your relationship with Kelly. I really like her for you. She's known our family all these years and has always adored you.

I'm sure you will make the right decision. Kelly knows the Lord and wants nothing more than to see you take that all important step and allow Jesus into your heart. I'm glad you're thinking about it. That's better than nothing. We're still praying for that day, just as we prayed we would all see you again.

I can see you have hang-ups about accepting the Lord. You may have heard this before, but God isn't mad

LETTERS FROM SECLUSION

at you. When you love a person as much as God loves you, it makes Him sad, not mad. He wants to have a personal relationship with you and is waiting for the day when you will.

Don't think you're not good enough to become a Christian. The smiling faces in church, you mentioned, doesn't mean anything. People will put up a front and pretend nothing is wrong in their lives, but the reality is, we all have struggles that consume us.

There's no rule that says we have to be perfect to be accepted by God. If that were the case, none of us would inherit the Kingdom. We all are guilty of sin and failures. That's exactly why we need Jesus. He died for you and me so we don't have to experience eternal damnation. As it says in John 3:16, For God so loved the world that He gave His only begotten Son, so that whoever believes in Him will not perish, but have eternal life.

I'm not trying to preach to you like a pastor. I'm sure you're thinking I'm in no position to quote scriptures to you. You know what? You're right. I'm not worthy of that or His amazing grace. That's what is so incredible about his unconditional love. He loved me even when I conceived you outside of marriage.

Since I'm on the subject of having you with a man I wasn't married to, let me clarify something. I didn't have your sisters with multiple men. They all have the same father. You know that. I told you that when you were a young boy. I didn't lie to you.

Let's move on to another subject. I'm glad you decided to stay a while longer. Rebecca told me you were headed back to Washington today. I would think you would say goodbye before you go. I know you have a home there and a job to go back to for the time being.

Since things are, as you say, falling apart in Washington, you will have to consider whether or not that's where God wants you to spend the rest of your life.

When your life crumbles all around you, it's a good indication you're not doing something right. Give it some time and pray for His guidance. I'm not talking to the air. This is the real thing.

Your family loves you. It may not feel that way, but you can't make decisions based on feelings. You've heard this from us all over the years. I won't go through it again.

I look forward to seeing you today,

Mom

LETTERS FROM SECLUSION

Mother,

It's weird sitting here writing letters back and forth while you're in the room, but I understand. I pray for the day when you can talk on your own. I see it's nap time, as your eyes are drooping closed. It happened in good time, because Kelly just came in.

Maybe you're faking going to sleep so you can eavesdrop on our conversation. Don't worry…we will step out after a while. No, I won't tell her I can't be with her. She's too beautiful and I love her dearly.

My heart is beating out of my chest,

Rich

Kelly,

I'm glad you came and took the time to visit with mom. She thinks the world of you. I think she would adopt you if she could. I'm really glad she didn't. I couldn't date my half-sister, or whatever you would call it.

We spent the entire walk from mom's room to the cafeteria in silence. I guess I'll have to speak first.

I spent most of the day alone after a sleepless night. I have some big decisions to make. I don't want to leave you. I've had enough of saying goodbye to you, for us to only talk through letters. I'm sure you've been praying I will break up with Sheila and date you. That's exactly what I want to talk to you about.

Now that we're seated in the cafeteria, let me start by saying I really love you. It's hard to eat right now as I wipe my sweaty palms on my pants. I'll calm myself.

I've had a great time with Sheila, but I now see she doesn't fulfill me. You make me feel like a man should. I can kick myself for letting all those years go by without loving you. I'm an idiot.

I see the smile on your face now. Were you really worried? In all honesty, I thought about going

314

back to Washington for good, but I just can't imagine life without you.

There's one hang-up I have. You've talked to me about being equally yoked. If I don't accept the Lord, will you not pursue a relationship with me? That puts a lot of pressure on me. I'm still struggling with it. I don't know how a God who's all powerful and can see everything I've done would want me in His family. No one has accepted me before…only you.

I'm not sure why you love me after all the harsh things I've said to you. I'm grateful, but I don't see how you can open your heart to me. I feel like I've made too many mistakes and hurt too many people to deserve love.

I know I sound like I'm feeling sorry for myself, but I could kick myself for being so stubborn all those years. I was so wrapped up in my problems that I didn't see…well…God's blessings.

There…I said it. There has to be a God who loves me if He can give me such supportive people, including the woman I've secretly loved for over 20 years.

Now I don't know what to say…accept I'm sorry. Also, I promise to always love you,

Rich

Sweet Rich,

Don't bury your face in your hands. You look like an ostrich. Are you so embarrassed to tell me you messed up that you can't look at me? That's silly. I love you the way you are. As long as you're willing to work on your issues, God will help you grow. It will be a long journey, but it's worth the trip.

God created you for His purposes. The enemy puts the thoughts in your head that you're not good enough to be loved. That's what made you flee to Washington. He had you where he wanted you for a season, but praise God, that season is over.

Believe it or not, I have a long way to go in my walk with the Lord. Don't look so surprised. If I thought I had it all together without any room to grow, I'd become one of those *holier-than-thou's*. Those people get on my nerves. They give themselves full authority to judge everyone else. I've learned when we spend too much time criticizing others, we can't look at ourselves and

316

analyze what we need to change. The very first thing would be our judgmental nature.

We really need to talk about something you mentioned. Sorry for the long pause, but you may not like what I have to say, even though you mentioned it. We do need to be equally yoked. It's important for many reasons. The first scripture that comes to mind is 2 Corinthians 6:14, *Do not be unequally yoked with unbelievers. For what partnership has righteousness with lawlessness? Or what fellowship has light with darkness?*

I could go all day quoting scriptures, but I wanted to bring this one up because it mentions the 'unequally yoked' we've been talking about, and it references 'partnership.' Our relationship that would eventually lead to marriage is a partnership. If we want God to bless it, we have to do things His way.

I don't want to pressure you into accepting the Lord if your heart isn't leading you in that direction. I know the Holy Spirit is tugging at your heart. He's the part of the Trinity that guides and leads us into the right direction. Only you can make the decision to accept Him.

I know I sound preachy. You've probably gotten enough of that from your mother and sister. I love them. They are so blunt, but say things out of love. I pray you see that now. Your family will never give up on you.

I hate to change the subject, but there's a brunette staring at you. Do you know her? She's been looking at you for a few minutes. Maybe she just thinks you're good looking. I can definitely understand that.

Maybe you can spread some light,

Suspicious Kelly

LETTERS FROM SECLUSION

Kelly,

With widened eyes, I see it's Sheila. I didn't invite her here. She came when I told her not to. She can't afford the trip. I don't know what to say to her after the couple weeks I've been away.

We wrote only once and I haven't called her at all. She's probably thinking my family is harassing me to no end. Be prepared for her to come in with fighting fists. Honestly, I was complaining to her about Rebecca and mom when we spoke a week ago. She's also going to be mad at me for not talking to her every day, as I promised.

Here she comes. I hope she doesn't fly off the handle in the middle of this cafeteria. I'm sorry you're forced to see all this.

Eyes widened,

Rich

Distant Rich,

Before you say anything, I want you to know I came because you haven't replied to my letters or called me in days. It's not like you to ignore me. Now I find you with this woman. I happen to see you here when I was searching the hospital for you. I figured you may stop here for some lunch, and I was right.

You should know I'm not one to give up. I was so worried your family was verbally abusing you that I couldn't help but come here. The suspense of waiting for you to tell me what's going on was overwhelming. I paid more money than I can afford to fly here and take a bus.

I don't want to fight as soon as I see you, but why haven't I heard from you? Is this woman the reason you forgot me? What's going on?

Demanding answers,

Sheila

Bad Timing Sheila,

I knew you would do this. Don't make a scene, please. I have been so busy and going through a host of emotions and I didn't know how to respond to you. I didn't want to bother you with every little detail.

Don't look so suspicious. Good grief...I was hoping for a better welcome when I saw you again. Okay...I understand it shocked you when you saw me with a woman. We should go somewhere and talk...alone.

Now that we're outside, I'll answer all your questions. That woman I was eating lunch with is Kelly. She's the old friend I told you about. I'm sorry I never told you she's a woman.

You're interrupting everything I'm saying. Can I finish one sentence...please? I guess not. Okay, I admit, I have feelings for her and she feels the same. We've been in love with each other since high school, but never talked about it. I didn't cheat on you...well, only in an emotional way.

I'm sorry you had to find out this way, but at least you know the truth. You came all this way because you were worried. I feel bad. Don't hate me.

FORGIVENESS IS A CHOICE

Transitioning back to Kansas City is a possibility. My job in Washington will end soon. It's inevitable. I missed Kelly the whole time I've been away, even though I dated you.

I know you're hurt…and I'm sorry. I will pay for your flight home and reimburse you for your travel. I know it doesn't make up for the pain.

Let's hug before we part,

Rich

Unfaithful Rich,

You have a lot of nerve, asking me to hug you after telling me all this. I waited and waited...and for what? I came here thinking you'd have a big smile on your face from missing me. Instead, I see you messing around with another woman.

So, you told me about her...big deal. You told me she was only a friend and I was under the impression it was a man. With a name like Kelly, I guess I should have known it was convenient for you to hide her gender. You men are all alike.

I hate to ask how long this has been going on. With my luck, you'll tell me you've been sending love letters back and forth for months. Don't say anything. I don't want to know.

Don't bother paying my way. I've been taking care of myself for years. I don't need your help now. I'll find the first flight back to Seattle on my own.

Please don't follow me,

Betrayed Sheila

FORGIVENESS IS A CHOICE

Rebecca,

I'm sorry I didn't come back to mom's room after lunch. I had a surprise visit from Sheila that didn't end well, as I'm sure you can imagine. Kelly was proud of me for telling her the truth. I'm not sure it was the right time or place to break that news, especially after she made the costly effort to come see me.

I feel like a pile of crap. Now Sheila added me to her list of worthless men. I really didn't need that after all I've been through these days. At least it's over and I'll never see her again. That's the way you wanted it.

I wanted to head to the bar after she left, but I left Kelly in the cafeteria. It goes without saying that Kelly wouldn't let me go on a drinking spree. I'm sure there will be a day when I'll be grateful. Now I feel like everyone and everything is stressing me out, no matter what I do.

I hope mom is doing okay. You didn't come bursting out your bedroom door, like a mad woman, when I came in. That tells me nothing earth shattering happened.

I have been praying a lot for mom, Sheila, and for God to reveal Jesus' face. I hope all of you haven't been wasting your time going to church, studying the Bible, and going on all those events with the church, etc. I'd like to think there is a God out there who loves me.

I'm sitting on the fence still. I'm embarrassed about some of the things I've done in my life and I know God saw all of it. This is the same God I'm supposed to ask for salvation. Can He really love me enough? I've sinned so much and deliberately rebelled against Him and my family.

I have to belong somewhere. I've tried so many venues in an attempt to fit in. Since I've been back to Kansas City, the "fitting in" seemed to find me. I'm not just talking about Kelly, although I'm still stunned about her. I would have never guessed she was just as in love with me as I am with her.

Now I have to try to sleep after another stressful day,

Rich

Little bro, Rich,

I can't help but smile as I read your letter this morning. My spirit is uplifted. Do you know why? You may not realize it, but you have grown to have a faith. The questions you keep asking show you admit God exists and He is all knowing. Don't worry about your past. He understands what you've been through and the mistakes you've made. What matters is the learning experience you take away from it.

I don't mean to sound sharp, but you got to get over your hang-up about your past. God is more interested in changing your heart. Only He can make that miraculous change in you, just as He did in me, mom, and everyone else who accepted the Lord Jesus Christ.

As for Sheila. I'm sorry she was hurt, but I knew she would be. Her heart will ache for a while...then it will heal. The best thing you can do for her now is pray for her soul. She will never have peace until she chooses to follow Jesus. That's not something you can do for her. It's her choice.

You've been a blessing in her life, for a season. Now that season is over and it's time for you to focus on Rich's life. Your responsibility is with your family and Kelly.

I know you have to go back to Washington to settle your house and transition from your old job into a new one. Perhaps you can go back to your company in downtown Kansas City. We all will be praying for God's favor on that. Your boss there really liked you and hated to see you go. You know that.

Mom smiled when I told her you chose Kelly over Sheila. Mom has always adored Kelly. It's a struggle for her to move her body or even make a face, but I saw a distinct smile out of her.

The doctors tell me she's progressing really well. It's astounding how she's able to talk some, which is improving. Through physical therapy, she was able to move 3 fingers today. It brought tears to my eyes.

All the prayers are working. No one can tell me there is no God, or He doesn't care about us. I know He's alive and more powerful than any medical condition. We won't give up on mom and you shouldn't either.

I know you two have had your problems in the past, but she needs to see as much of you as she can. Is

LETTERS FROM SECLUSION

it possible for you to stay 1 more week? I think seeing you again has given her the strength to fight. I don't mean to put pressure on you, but it's really how I feel.

Well, I'm off to work now. Go see our mother and hug Kelly for me,

Rebecca

Son,

It's good to see you again this morning. I hear you and Kelly are working things out. I'm so happy for you both. That Sheila isn't right for you. She works in a bar and doesn't know the Lord. That bothers a mother...even a mother who isn't worth the title "mom."

Sometimes I feel like I've wasted my whole adult life with bitterness. It kept me from loving you the way you deserved. It robbed you of a safe childhood. Most of all, it robbed us both of the mother-son relationship. I was a fool.

Forgiveness is one of the hardest things to do. I'm not asking you to forgive for my sake. I don't want to be let off the hook. There's something more important...your joy and peace. Every minute you walk around with unforgiveness in

LETTERS FROM SECLUSION

your heart, the devil laughs, because he knows it keeps you from your walk with the Lord.

Even Christians, who have loved God with their whole hearts, are missing out on their blessings, because they refuse to let go of the pain inflicted by others. It's time to lay it down at the foot of the cross and let Him take it away.

If you will try to do that, I can work toward forgiving your father and myself. We don't have to walk around with that evil. Unforgiveness leads to hatred. 1 John 3:15 says: Anyone who hates a brother or a sister is a murderer, and you know that no murderer has eternal life residing in him.

You see...we must forgive each other so we can live the life of Christ and enter into His Kingdom. That shows how important it is.

FORGIVENESS IS A CHOICE

The pain I caused you wasn't your fault, it was my doing. This was something that happened **to** you, not **because** of you. The same goes for that man who took advantage of my vulnerability. Yes, I chose to fall into sin, but he had no intentions of staying with me in the long run. He lied and manipulated me. I was partially a victim, even though it happened because of my sin. I have to own up to that.

All this sounds real complicated, and it is. I want you to understand something. Holding unforgiveness isn't worth losing our salvation. When we hold a grudge, we are giving that person or people who hurt us the power to steal our joy. Now, that has to give you something to think about.

After saying all this, I want to ask you to pray about all this, just as I will. The Lord will work it out if we are both willing to love each other from this day forward.

Please take what I'm saying to heart,

Praying Mom

Ex-Boyfriend, Rich,

I don't know where to start. The plane ride was a long one. It wasn't easy to hold back my tears. I'm angry and really, really hurt. I can't believe my first visit to Kansas City was such a disaster. I could smack you.

I just finished work. It was the longest shift I ever worked. All I could think about was you. The entire tavern has something that reminds me of you and all the talks we had. I can still remember the first time you talked to me, in your timid way. Then when I brought you all those many margaritas, you stiffened up and blushed as we made eye contact.

All the memories that used to make me smile, now make me ache. I have to say goodbye to you and go back to that dead-end job I hate. I won't be able to sleep one wink tonight or any other night for a while.

I had a guy pinch me tonight. Then he wouldn't let go of my leg. I have no choice but to pretend I enjoy perverts like him, so I make good tip money. It really makes me want to crawl into a hole and die. I can't stomach the idea of doing this for the rest of my life...I'm stuck.

LETTERS FROM SECLUSION

There's no future for me to look forward to. No man who loves me and no way of pursuing my dream of owning a beauty salon and raising a family. Who wants to date a bartender except drunken perverts?

I had such high hopes with you. I don't want to say you turned out like all the rest, but you really did. I caught you cheating with an old girlfriend. You never even mentioned her. What am I supposed to do with that?

As for your family...I don't know where to start. Those Christians are all the same. I told you that way back in the beginning. You can't trust them. They're all hypocrites who judge you, use you, then stab you in the back.

Look at what they've done. They destroyed our wonderful relationship. Things were going so well. You made me laugh and lifted my spirits like no other man could do. What was it all for? I miss you already. Don't let them keep you away from me. I can't help but think we were made for each other. Don't let it end this way...please.

I have to lay down and try to forget about you...at least for now. It will be impossible, but I

335

must live what little life I have with this thug roommate of mine.

I'm sorry for sounding angry. I don't mean to bite your head off, but I had to get my feelings out there. The truth is the truth.

I don't know if I'll ever hear from you again. If not, so long,

Broken-Hearted Sheila

Rebecca,

I just got mom's latest letter. I'm sure you wrote it out for her, since she can't write. Apparently, she's been talking better over the last few days. Sorry, I've been away. I want to spend as much time with Kelly as I can while she is off work. We'll be by after lunch.

Mom had some deep things to say. Kelly read her letter and we talked about it for most of the day yesterday. She convinced me I had to change my way of thinking. It's only hurting myself. I've been really selfish…I admit it…yes.

I'm overwhelmed by the response I've had over the last couple of weeks. Danielle came over your place today to see me. I was shocked to see her emotional. That's not something I've ever seen, I don't think. She gave me a big hug and told me she loved me. It felt good to hug that old lady…he-he.

She got up early and swung by just to see me before she headed to work. All the years of her picking on me didn't matter anymore. The past is over.

She kept telling me how much she wanted me to stay and be a part of the family again. Then she invited me over her house for dinner this evening.

I laughed when she said, "I insist you bring Kelly." I guess she likes her too. What's not to like. Kelly is wonderful.

All of this is really overwhelming. I don't know where to start. There's still the Sheila problem. She's really mad at me. I feel bad for breaking her heart. I'm a heathen. I don't know if I should respond to her latest letter. It might make her angrier.

Then there's the issue of my house in Washington. I'll have to sell it…or maybe I can use it for a vacation home. What do you think? I don't have to ask. You'll tell me what to do anyway. That's what big sisters are for. I'm sure you will agree.

What about my job. I can't just pack up and leave. They rely on me. I have to find a new job back home. Maybe I can go back to my old company downtown. They told me I could go back, but that was a long time ago.

What to do…what to do,

Shaking Rich

Rich,

Cool it, little Bro! The first thing you need to do is calm down. Some things never change. You get so worked up about everything. Let's take it one step at a time.

Before you do anything, mom needs to see you. She's talking better. The number one thing she wants right now is to have a conversation with her son. It's been too many years since you two have talked. Please take the time to do that today. I want to see you in her hospital room today...bring Kelly.

Forget about Sheila. I'm sure she is heart-broken, but she will live. Women are full of emotion. Trust me, it will pass. She will find the right man who will hopefully straighten her out. She sure needs it. You have no reason to feel guilty. Some relationships work and others don't. It's a part of life.

You need to focus on your life. It's changing for the better. As you say, there are lots of things you need to take care of. Now...listen to me on this. You don't have to be in a dire hurry. Your house will still be there and it takes time to sell. Don't stress yourself out...relax.

With your experience, finding another job will be a cinch. If I were you, I wouldn't worry about hanging onto your old job out of loyalty. You've been loyal enough. It's time for you to take care of yourself. That's more important. That company you work for, whoever they are, will survive. You told me your work has been slaking anyway. If that continues, they may lay you off, along with dozens of other employees. So much for loyalty.

That's my opinion and I'm sticking to it. You decide what's best for you. Don't let Sheila put things in your head about your family. I'm sure she did already. She doesn't know any of us, so how can she judge?

Get your butt to the hospital and have a nice evening with Danielle,

Rebecca

My dear son, Rich,

It's so good to see you. I'm sorry you have to see the nurse feeding me lunch. It may be that way for a while. My hands don't work so well. At least, I can wipe my own face...kind of.

You finally came to your senses and got together with Kelly. She's been waiting too many years for you to admit you like her. Actually, I think you love her. She sure loves you...and always has.

It hurts a little to breathe, so be patient with me through my breathiness. My back is hurting too. I guess it's a good sign that I feel pain. It means I'm still alive.

Well...I don't know what to say. I prayed about being able to talk to you again and now I'm at a loss for words. It's a miracle you're here.

LETTERS FROM SECLUSION

I want to say, "I'm sorry again," but it won't help how you feel. It won't bring back all the time we lost. It won't erase the mistakes I made. I'm sorry to cry in front of you and Kelly. It's embarrassing.

Confined Mom

Upset Mom,

You don't need to beat yourself up about it. I've been doing enough of beating myself up for the both of us. Don't cry. You know how I can't stand to see a woman cry. So, I'm a softy.

Kelly and I talked for hours about all of this. It was hard to admit my mistakes. Running away isn't the antidote for adversity. I had to learn a hard lesson in forgiving myself.

So, here's the next step. I want you to look at me when I say this. I forgive you. We can't erase the past, but with God's help, He will find a way to fix all this. Yes...I said, "God will fix it."

I'm not sure where to go from here with my faith. Kelly tells me Jesus loves me just the way I am. I'm so glad He does, because I have a hard time loving myself right now.

Danielle just came in to see all of us in tears. What a warm welcome, right? Now she's crying. I didn't mean to cause so much pain. I used to think no one would care if I left. I thought everyone would cheer when they realized I was gone. I was an idiot.

Rich

Rich,

I'm going to stop you there. You're not an idiot. I don't want to hear you say that again. You're my brother...the only one I have. Do you have any idea how precious that is to me? When I got word you were gone, it left a hole in my heart that nothing could fill.

I, too, need to apologize. I picked on you way too much when we were kids. I was jealous of your relationship with Rebecca. The bond you two have is irreplaceable. I had no right to be bitter with you. It was my problem.

I'm so glad you and Kelly hooked up. I was wondering if you would ever see how much she loves you. You know, she's like family without the wedding vows. Her family and ours have been friends since you two were in high school. How awesome is that? At least, we know there won't be any in-law issues.

I don't mean to push you down the altar. I'll just say, get your stubborn butt over to my house tonight for dinner. We have a lot to talk about.

Relieved,

Danielle

Mom,

Now that everyone is gone, I want to talk to you a while longer. I keep pondering the same thing in my mind. There was a time when I was so angry, I wanted to bomb Kansas City. Now I realize I was irrational, to say the least. I can't believe I was such a cold-blooded jerk.

I hated God…or believed there couldn't be one. It was all because of my embarrassment. I was so full of pride, I couldn't accept Rebecca seeing me on my living room floor in a drunken stupor. The only thing I could think about was running and hiding.

Our conversations over the past few years has been focused on your mistakes. I couldn't see my mistakes. I was blind. I won't call myself an idiot. I got yelled at once today for that.

My question to you is this. Where do we go from here? I want to have a relationship with you again, but I don't want things to be awkward. Can we let go of the past? Is it possible?

Sorry I'm shifting in my seat. There's another, more important question I want to ask. I want to have a relationship with Jesus. Kelly talked to me for hours and read scriptures to me. My eyes were nodding, we talked so long. She said something about the sinner's prayer, but I declined. I'm still not sure I have a pure enough heart.

The way I've been living hasn't worked. Working long hours and drinking half the night, 7 days a week, is killing me. I had no idea how much I abused myself.

Help me out here,

Rich

Son,

That day I've been praying about has arrived. Help me sit up. It's been a few weeks since I've been able to sit like a normal person. Thanks. That's better.

You don't have to be perfect to accept the Lord. I'm far from sinless. God loves me and He's working on me. I'm not where I need to be in my walk with Christ, but praise God I'm not where I used to be. If he can love me, He can love you...and does.

No one can force you to follow Jesus Christ. It's a decision you need to make on your own. Don't worry about what you've done. Concern yourself with the present. This is the day you make the right choice.

It's the most important decision you will ever make, Rich. He came to earth and died for the sins of many. If you were the only person in the entire world to accept Christ, He still would have died for you. That shows how much he loves you.

It doesn't take much to have a personal relationship with Christ. If you're ready to pick up your cross and follow Him, repeat after me. Don't be shy. Sit next to me and take my hand, son.

Father God...thank you for loving me. I admit, I am a sinner. I have fallen short of Your glory. I need you, now more than ever. Lord Jesus, come into my heart. Change me into who you want me to

LETTERS FROM SECLUSION

be. Holy Spirit, teach me and guide me...convict me. I want to be more like you. I pray all this in Jesus name...amen.

Hug me son. I'm so proud of you. Your sisters are all here, along with Kelly. They came in a few minutes ago. We're all proud of the man you've become.

A group hug is in order,

Mom

Sneaky Mom,

You knew everyone was watching and listening to me pray with you with my eyes closed. That was slick. Now I'm being smothered to death. Enough group hugging. Breathing is essential.

I never felt so loved in all my life. I guess that was all part of God's plan. This must be the divine intervention Kelly told me about.

Now we all need to pray for your full recovery. I want to see you home, sleeping in your own bed. That is…if everyone can stop crying long enough to do so.

Life is good,

Rich

Despairing Sheila,

I contemplated whether I should write you. I don't want to raise more ill feelings. If it does, I'm sorry. Well, here it goes.

I'm not angry at your last letter, but sad that I hurt you. The time we spent together was special. You don't have to feel that you failed at another relationship. That's just not true.

I know you don't like to talk about faith, but the Lord was calling me and watching me while I made bad decisions and suffered the consequences. I understand some things happened to me that were out of my control. I was hurt by people who should have loved me. It was the source of the problems that prompted me to move away.

It's a thing of the past now. I had to forgive them just as Christ has forgiven me. The grudges I held hurt me much more than it hurt them. I lost my peace and joy. How did I cope with the bitterness and pain? I attempted to close myself off from the rest of the world…just me and my alcohol.

I quickly learned it's impossible to avoid people altogether…they're everywhere. That old man I befriended seemed like a nice guy and a good mentor. The truth is, he has more problems than I have. Our backgrounds were similar, which is

351

why we got along so well. We had lots to talk about…always.

I allowed him to fill my head with all kinds of garbage about how people use you and stab you in the back. I believed it all, hence the reason I moved to Washington in the first place. We both wallowed in our misery together with as much alcohol we could consume in one night, just to do it again the next day.

My drinking didn't begin there. I started drinking under age with my friends in high school. I wanted to "fit in," as they say, so I thought it was cool. All these friends I hung with ended up turning on me eventually.

I knew Kelly back then. She wasn't involved with my drinking. She used to get mad at me when I did foolish things. I knew she cared for me back then, but I was a blind teenager who only thought about myself. I couldn't see how much she loved me, even then.

It used to annoy me when she ragged me about my drinking. All I could think of was how she sounded like my sister, so I got mad. I wasn't the most approachable person…heck…I wasn't approachable as an adult. I put up brick walls around me when I was told things I didn't want to hear.

The point is, I had been hurt by my mother and sisters, abandoned by my father, and now betrayed by almost every friend I had in school. It's a lot to stomach for a 15 or 16-year-old. None of it mattered, since I usually anticipated being moved to another foster home. No one ever adopted me.

I know I'm reiterating everything, but I'm telling you all this for a reason. I may have been mistreated in many ways, with times where I felt like no one wanted me, but God was watching me. He knew there would be a day I would open my eyes and see the truth about Jesus.

When I was looking down a deep, dark hole, He had his healing hands on me. I didn't know it, but the Lord was there to pick me up and help me to my feet again. When there seemed to be no way out of my depression, God did a miracle in me and changed my heart, in His time.

You can do what you want with the things I'm telling you. It's up to you to accept Jesus or not. I can't make that decision for you. I pray you take my words to heart. I care for you enough to tell you things you don't want to hear. If I was there, I'd give you a big hug right now.

I'm sure by now, you've seen the Bible I enclosed with this letter. Please take the time to read it and get into a good Bible based church. They're around. Also, there's a small envelope with my old house key inside. You are welcome to stay there as long as you like. This way, you don't have to live with your wacked out roommate anymore. Don't worry about paying me rent.

Last, there's a flat envelope with a certified check in it. This should cover your tuition and books for the next two years. You can go to that beauty school you and I talked about. It's on me. I want you to succeed.

They have classes during the day, so you can still work at the tavern at night. It will work out perfectly with your work schedule. I've done my research, so I know it's possible for you to work and take classes. Stay focused and fulfill your dream.

Kelly knows I've done this for you. She's very supportive and wants to see you better yourself too. We prayed about it together and felt the Lord leading us to assist you. You can thank God, not me.

Now, there's only one more thing to address. Our past relationship. As I've said, it wasn't a failure. You filled my heart with laughter and lifted my spirits. It was all part of God's plan that we met. Don't think it was all for nothing. The right man is out there. Lots of prayers are coming your way.

354

Focus on your future and on God. He loves you more than words can say. Jesus is waiting for you to hold out your hand and reach for Him. He desires to have a personal relationship with you. All you have to do is ask. Give God a chance.

Blessings to you now and always,

Rich

Supportive Kelly,

I did it. I don't know if Sheila will accept the money or the Lord, but at least it's done. I hate to bother you with this now. Sheila should be a thing of the past. This should put closure to it.

It was so good of you to allow me to pay for her beauty school. It shows how wonderful you are. I wish I said this sooner...much sooner.

Now, I'm heading to my old house to clean out my furniture and stinky underwear. Fortunately, I didn't have much in there. That house is so dark, mainly because I kept the dark drapes closed at all times. It helped keep me in seclusion. Those days are gone, praise the Lord.

I'll be back in a few days. Mom will be coming home soon, so I must get back and move in with her for now. She needs someone to take care of her until she fully recovers. You can guess who was elected. I don't mind. In fact, it's long overdue.

I'll look for a job after a while. Mom needs to feel comfortable with being alone at home first. I hope we don't get on one another's nerves too bad. I worry too much.

The anxiety is heightening.

Anyway, I'll see you in a few days.

I love you,

Rich

My dear son, Rich,

I'm coming home soon. I hope you will make it back to the hospital in time to pack my stuff up and get your old mother to the house. I hate it that you're stuck taking care of me. Don't feel obligated, son. My insurance will pay for home health for as long as I need it.

I'm not crazy about the idea of having nurses coming in and out all hours of the night, but I will consider it. You don't have to take care of me just because you've been away for so long. You have nothing to feel guilty about. We've had this conversation.

I'm happy for you and Kelly. You finally found love. It was long overdue. I'm smiling while your sister writes this letter for me. A mother wants her children to be happy. Maybe you'll let me plan your wedding. I'm excited at the thought of it.

By God's grace, you ended up back where you belong, with the family He's given you. I've never told you this before, but I'm proud of you. The man you've become in business gives me something to brag about. I can't wait to tell all my friends and the extended family.

Your ability to forgive the unforgivable can only come from the Lord. I will praise Him for ever more. Through the gift of your son, Jesus Christ, I finally have my son back. Thank you for wiping the slate clean.

I look forward to wrapping my arms around you soon,

Mom

Jumping the gun, Mom,

You're so funny. Kelly and I just got together and you've got us married already. Slow down. Kelly and I haven't talked about that at all. How about you let us make the plans for now? That sounds like a better idea.

I talked to my old boss. He's going to allow me to come back. I'll be working for the same company, but my position isn't available. They hired a man who's been a CEO for several companies. Oh well. I couldn't expect him to hold my job all these years. I'm glad I have employment.

Taking care of you will not be a burden. Don't worry about it. I look forward to getting to know my mother again, as well as my sisters. It'll be more like getting to know you for the first time.

I don't have to go away to another strange family again. My biological family is strange enough. I wouldn't trade them for anything in the world. It's a little awkward, but I'd rather be here than Washington, any day of the week.

Rebecca already arranged for Home Health Services to come over to your house. They will stop by whenever you need them. At first, they will be by 3 times a day or more. As you recover, it will be less often.

FORGIVENESS IS A CHOICE

I know you…you will be stubborn about having them there. I'm not listening to any of it. They do this for a living and will be more than happy to take care of you.

I guess I will move back into my old room for now…which was the den. I'm used to a room without windows. In the Washington house, I covered all the windows with black drapes. The privacy created loneliness, but at least I could work without distractions.

When I get back, Kelly and I will invite everyone over for dinner. It will be good for everyone to see you out of the hospital. I'm not sure where we will seat everyone, but Kelly is a good coordinator. You, my 4 sisters, and Kelly will be under 1 roof. I don't know if I can handle all that estrogen in one evening.

Well…I'm off to settle things here in Washington. I should only be here another day or two. Then it's my final one-way trip to Kansas City.

It was a long journey, full of pain and uncertainty. I drank and cried…then I drank and cried again. In the end, the pain was still there. So, I drank some more, until I was falling over drunk. It's amazing I was able to drive in that condition. It took an act of God to keep me and others on the road safe.

Speaking of which, God moved in my life in ways I can't explain. I didn't want to admit He existed. The reality is, I was angry with Him. The problem was, I tried to handle things in my own strength. Stubbornness is one of my strongholds. I was too full of pride to lean on Him and accept that I can't make it on my own.

The Lord's faithfulness brought me through, even though I had no idea what He was doing. When I said He was dead, he knew one day I would come alive. One drop of Jesus' blood wiped my sins away, but He spilled it all out anyway.

I'm overwhelmed at how much He loves me,

Rich

Blessed Son,

It's good to hear you speak of Jesus' love. It is overwhelming how faithful He is, even when we aren't. You make this mother smile. It's been a long time since I've been able to.

I knew you would get your old job back. They knew you were the best of the best and I'm sure they are rejoicing to see you are coming back. See...it's not just your family who missed you. I'm sure it won't be long before you get your old position back. You're the best CEO money can buy.

I don't see how you can hold a job, have a girlfriend, and take care of me full time. You're going to have enough on your mind, son. I'll keep my mouth shut about the home health people. They better not treat me like an invalid. I pray Jesus will heal me quickly.

You better get used to "all that estrogen." You will be surrounded by it from now on. Don't forget, you're the only male in this family, until you give me grandsons. Not to push things on you, but I'd like nothing more than to see you happy with the girl of your dreams. You and I both know Kelly has been on your mind since you two met in high school. A mother knows.

By the time you read this letter, everyone will have come for your and Kelly's big dinner. I can't tell you how blessed I am to finally have all my children and their families in this house again. Seeing

362

all you sitting at this dining room table makes me realize how gracious and merciful the Lord is.

I don't deserve any of this after all the mistakes I've made. I could have been a better mom. Things would have turned out different if I didn't make that mistake to sleep with your father when we weren't married, but the biggest blessing God pulled out of it was you. A child is never a mistake...especially when it's my child.

Praise You Heavenly Father. Your mercies are new every day. I have come short of Your glory. With all my mistakes, You forgave me...You saw me through all my pain and emptiness. You answered my prayers and brought my son back. Glory to your Holy Name! Thank you, Jesus...my Lord and my God!

His promises are true, now and forever!

Mom

www.ingramcontent.com/pod-product-compliance
Lightning Source LLC
Chambersburg PA
CBHW071514260626
47170CB00002B/361